I0676440

SEASON of MADNESS

AIRSHIP 27 PRODUCTIONS

Season of Madness

Published by Airship 27 Productions
Airship27.com
Airship27Hangar.com

"Season of Madness" and "Attack of the Electric Shark" © copyright 2009 Aaron Smith
Interior llustrations © 2009 Pedro Cruz
Cover © 2009 Rob Davis and Shane Evans

Editor: Ron Fortier
Associate Editor: Charles Saunders
Production and design: Rob Davis.

All rights reserved under International and Pan-American Copyright
Conventions. No part of this book may be reproduced in any manner without
permission in writing from the copyright holder, except by a reviewer, who
may quote brief passages in a review.

ISBN-13: 978-0692564929 (Airship 27)
ISBN-10: 0692564926

Printed in the United States of America

10 9 8 7 6 5 4 3 2 1

Contents

Season of Madness
(A Doctor Watson Adventure)

With Holmes away on a foreign assignment, it falls to Dr. Watson and his ally, Dr. Seward, to discover the cause of madness sweeping over London and end the threat before it can infect the entire country.

SPECIAL BONUS FEATURE
"Attack of the Electric Shark"
(A Hound Dog Harker Adventure)

Introducing Quincy Harker of Her Majesty's Secret Service in the first of a brand new adventure series. Harker and his friends face danger on the high seas as a long-lost ship of scientific marvels returns to challenge all of mankind.

Chapter I:
Madness Gathers 'Round

It was a fairly typical mid-morning in the autumn in London when the first sign of the scattered madness first caught the attention of the people. The streets were busy, as they always were in that part of the city; people bustling back and forth, some on their way to or from the places at which they were employed, others shopping or otherwise going about their business.

The crowd moved along the streets, some intermittent rudeness punctuating the flow of foot traffic, but the people were, as usual, moderately polite and mostly concerned only with their own comings and goings. Then came the voice, louder than all the others, booming from somewhere among the mass of pedestrians, audible over even the clopping of the horses' hooves and the harsh rolling sound of the hansom wheels.

"Get moving, people! Move! Move along!"

The man in the top hat began to shove his way through the crowd, first startling an older gentleman with a rude passing jostle. He came bursting through the crowd, his movements growing cruder and more violent with each step.

Some of the people turned to see who was causing all the commotion. They were greeted by the sight of a tall man in his thirties, built like a boxer, with thick bushy sideburns. His face was a purposeful scowl and he barked like a guard dog as he pushed and shoved.

"Outta the way, you bloody fool! Imbeciles, all of you! Make way! Some of us have plans of great importance to carry out! Move, you bloody idiots!"

Another man, younger, and well dressed, stepped into the path of the rude, hurried man. He put up his hands as if to signal the rude one to stop his obnoxious behavior.

"Please, sir," he asked, "There is no reason to act in such a manner. You, sir, are in the presence of gentlemen and ladies. A bit of discretion and a gentler tone of voice would serve just as well."

The man in the top hat punched him square in the face. Shock was apparent on the younger man's face as blood spurted from his nose. A woman standing nearby began to scream.

"Summon the police! Summon the police!" she cried.

The rude man flung his top hat to the ground in a display of further anger.

"This is intolerable! Let me be on my way!"

Two of London's police appeared on the scene, attracted by the noise and confusion.

"You, stop there, halt!" shouted the blue-coated officers of the law, grabbing hold of the large, rude man. They were quickly flung aside like small cloth dolls.

The residence of Alexander Bird and his family sat on the outskirts of London. It was a moderately sized, well kept home, one which passersby would correctly assume belonged to a well off, but not excessively affluent, family.

Night had come to London and those citizens who kept normal hours were mostly asleep for the evening. Alexander Bird had not been ready to retire for the night yet, so he had gone to his study for a few quiet hours with a book and a drink. The rest of the household, as far as he knew, were soundly sleeping, each in their respective quarters.

One floor above Alexander's study, his seventeen year old daughter, Clarice, suddenly awoke. She sat up in bed, feeling a sudden, irresistible urge to do something she had never done before. She pushed aside the blankets and sat up in bed. Her long, black hair fell around her shoulders as she stood. She did not reach for her robe, nor did she bother to stop for her slippers. She took a lamp from her bedside table and lit its wick. She went to her door, opened it, and stepped out into the hallway in her nightgown and bare feet.

She walked to the end of the hall and descended the staircase, not making any extraneous noise, but not being particularly careful to maintain quiet either. She had things on her mind other than consideration for her sleeping family members.

Within minutes she had reached the parlor. She entered and looked around, the room illuminated only by her lamplight. The parlor was typical of that of houses of the Bird residence's size in that part of London. The room contained several chairs, a couch, bookshelves along the walls, and a piano with its accompanying bench.

Clarice Bird placed the lamp atop the piano and sat down on the bench. Her slim fingers began to dance upon the keys and music, perfectly executed, began to stream forth from the instrument.

Upstairs in her own bedroom, Clarice's mother was stirred from sleep by the sound of those piano keys. The music was breathtakingly beautiful, ethereal and enchanting. She had never heard such music. She rose from her bed, threw on a robe and slippers and followed the trail of exquisite sounds, down the steps and into the parlor. Mrs. Bird gasped as she saw that her daughter was the source of the wondrous sound.

"Clarice, is that you? How are you doing that?" she said, amazed.

Clarice turned to look at her mother. She continued to play as she glanced over. The music did not stop.

"How am I doing what, Mother?"

"Clarice…the music," said her stunned mother. "You've never played like that before; not once!"

Clarice smiled, but it was not the charming smile that her mother was used to seeing from her daughter. It was a strange, serene, but oddly trance-like smile, like the expression of one who has been hypnotized.

"Mother…sometimes people change."

Mrs. Bird went pale. She was shocked by the emotionless way her daughter had just spoken to her.

"But you've never even been interested in that piano, Clarice," she said.

Clarice offered no further response. She turned back to the piano and kept playing, the music growing louder, stranger, but also more beautiful.

Mrs. Bird opened her mouth and screamed out her husband's name.

"Alexander! Alexander!"

In his study, Alexander Bird nearly fell out of his chair. He had been engrossed in a book of poems, blocking out all noise in the background, mesmerized by the beauty of the passages he had been reading. The solidly built gentleman with the neat graying beard spilled half of his drink and stood up quickly, surprised and worried by the panic in his wife's voice.

He ran to the parlor to find his wife standing in the doorway trembling and his daughter seated at the piano, still playing. The music caught Alexander's attention now and he stopped moving and just listened. His wife spoke.

"How is this happening? What does it mean?"

Alexander was too entranced to even attempt to answer his wife's question.

"Listen to her. It's beautiful," was all he could manage to say.

"What does it mean?" his wife demanded.

Alexander moved closer to the piano and his wife followed. They stood behind Clarice, the music still flowing from the piano as her fingers danced flawlessly across the keys. Alexander Bird finally uttered a response to his wife's repeated question.

"It means that we are witnessing either a miracle…or the work of the devil!"

The Carpathian Mountains stood, dark and foreboding, like a landscape from some subconscious memory, common to all members of the human race; the kind of place that would tend to spring up in nightmares. Snow was falling, joining the arrival of nightfall in those dreadful mountains. The gypsy-driven, horse-pulled cart had come to a halt. The wagon was surrounded and its attending Romanian gypsies defended themselves against those who stood against them and their master. Jonathan and Mina Harker, Abraham Van Helsing, Quincy Morris, Arthur Holmwood, and Dr. John Seward were all prepared to fight to the death against the thing in the coffin atop the carriage and its servants. Seward and Holmwood, armed with guns, held some of the gypsies in place with threats of bullets. Jonathan Harker and Quincy Morris battled their way through the remaining gypsies, surging towards the wagon and finally climbing atop the stilled vehicle. Morris was wounded, but his American fortitude would not be stopped. The lid was torn from the coffin. Inside laid the soon-to-awaken target of their crusade…Dracula, the wretched thing that had come to London and made their lives into a series of nightmares. Now they had pursued the vampire lord back there, to his homeland, and they intended to destroy him.

As the lid was torn away, the sun descended below the horizon. The vampire's eyes opened! His face turned into a malicious expression of pure hate and his pursuers knew that they had to strike swiftly and decisively. Harker's dagger sliced across Dracula's throat, while Morris's big Bowie knife plunged into the count's undead heart. Dracula's reign of terror and bloodshed was finally, mercifully, ended!

Dr. John Seward woke up. He could feel the hard surface of his desk under his forehead and he knew he had fallen asleep in his office again. Trying to wade through piles of reports had exhausted him and he had dozed off, only to relive that night in the Carpathians yet again. He stood and walked to his phonograph recording machine, which it was his habit to use to keep his diaries of both cases and personal thoughts. He started the recording process and began to speak.

"Being a doctor, particularly one of my specialties, I am fully aware of what dreams really are. Dreams are composed of bits of the mind's mysterious workings; a potent mosaic of memory, fantasy, thought, desire, fear, and whatever other debris accumulates in the head of a man. I know, with absolute intellectual certainty, that the events I keep reliving in my dreams are events of the past...gone by and never to be repeated in my lifetime, but they keep returning to haunt almost every night's rest, lingering as if I may never be rid of these horrible visions. We won our battle! The evil we sought out was indeed destroyed! But I wonder if that bloodthirsty monster has not gained some victory by taking up residence in our minds, never to be fully driven out."

The recording of his thoughts usually served to calm Seward's mind after such episodes and he retired to his bed and found himself able to sleep soundly for the rest of the night.

Morning arrived sooner than Seward would have liked. He felt rested, but not nearly as rested as would have restored him to the full vitality of the young man that he was. The lack of sleep since the Dracula ordeal had been wearing on him of late. He woke and soon returned to his office, where he added a few words to the previous night's phonographic journal entry.

"I have even gone so far as to write Professor Van Helsing, my mentor and friend, for advice. I thought perhaps his skill with hypnosis might bring me some rest...but he cannot come. He has gone to America on some business. Will there be no end to these damned dreams, no respite from the torment of recollection?"

Having just finished speaking his thoughts aloud to the machine, Seward was startled by a sudden knocking on his office door. The voice of his assistant and chief orderly, Sullivan, rang out.

"Doctor, Doctor Seward, are ye' in there?"

"Come in, Sullivan," Seward responded. "What is it?"

Sullivan walked into the office. He was a short, stocky man in his mid-forties. He had a look of urgent excitement on his swarthy face.

"Coppers just brought us a live one, Sir! Bloody mess 'e is, this one, Sir, a hell of a bloody mess!"

Seward stood up. He suddenly felt awake again, as if the news of a new patient had broken his tired, hopeless mood. He was already headed to the door as he replied to Sullivan's statement.

"What do you mean, 'a bloody mess,'? Explain, Sullivan, or better yet... take me to the man!"

As Seward was about to bolt through the door, Sullivan raised a hand to signal for him to wait.

"Just a minute, Sir, one o' the coppers insisted on speakin' to ya before you see the patient," Sullivan informed him. The orderly turned to the door and called out, "C'mon in, Inspector!"

The policeman entered, nodding to Sullivan and walking over to where Seward stood. He was a thin, ferret-like man of forty or so, in a typical non-uniformed policeman's overcoat, holding his derby in his left hand. He extended his right hand to greet Seward.

"Inspector Lestrade, Scotland Yard."

"This is a bit odd, Inspector," said Seward as the two men shook hands. "We're not used to having patients brought in by the police with no prior notice at all. Such an event can be made easier on all parties if a bit of preparation is made..."

Lestrade interrupted.

"I'm sorry, Doctor, but this isn't exactly an ordinary patient...if there's any such thing in a place such as this one!"

Seward could feel himself growing impatient with Lestrade's roundabout way of getting to the meat of the matter.

"Then explain, Inspector. Please."

Lestrade stepped around Seward and plopped himself down into a chair to the side of the desk.

"We got word of some commotion about two hours ago. It seems a shop clerk had gone runnin' out into the streets screamin' and cryin' for the police. One of our patrol constables, a fellow called Paddington, went to see what all the fuss was about."

As he spoke, Lestrade wiped his forehead with a handkerchief. Whatever had occurred that evening had clearly upset the inspector.

"When I got there," Lestrade continued, "I found poor Paddington sittin' on the front stoop, paler than a ghost and sick as an old hound dog. When I went through that shop door, I saw just why!"

Lestrade pulled a small notebook from his pocket and flipped it open. Seward, an avid observer of human behavior, knew that Lestrade had no real need to consult his notes, but was fumbling with the book to conceal the nervousness that this conversation was causing him. Seward let him do as he was doing and kept listening.

"The shop was run by a Mister...umm...here it is...Abner Cromwell, aged thirty-seven. I found him sitting in the shop, looking up and smiling a big smile when I walked in. There didn't seem to be anything wrong at first."

"Then I saw it; right in front of him on a little dinner plate. He asked if I was hungry...and he pointed at a plate of human fingers! He said he made them himself. Then I saw the condition of his right hand...and I knew just how he'd made them!"

"Dr. Seward, I've seen some horrible sights in my life; murder victims, all sorts of atrocities, and I'm not a weak man. This was different! It wasn't the sight of the blood and the fingers that got to me, Sir. It was the strange, weird joy in the man's eyes!"

"The whole time we had him there and at the stationhouse, he was smiling, singing, full of happiness. He's got to be insane, Doctor. There's no other way for a man to do a thing like that, is there? So...we called for a surgeon to stitch the poor loony up...and we brought him here to you."

Three days later, Dr. Seward once again turned on his phonograph machine to record his findings on the case of his newest patient, Abner Cromwell. After activating the machine, he sat at the desk to speak aloud to the recorder. As he sat, scraps of newspapers fell from the desk. It had been a strange few days for Seward and he was beginning to wonder if he might not be ready to join his patients in their little cells. He had been eagerly looking through each day's newspaper after first meeting Cromwell...and he was growing somewhat concerned about what he was finding in those papers.

"Patient: Abner Cromwell, aged thirty-seven; Dr. John Seward recording."

"I am beginning to fully agree with Inspector Lestrade's assessment. Perhaps Cromwell is, as Lestrade put it, quite loony. I have now spent several hours in interviews with the patient, Cromwell. I have never observed a happier individual...and it frightens me. I have not been this disturbed, but intrigued nevertheless, by a patient since the unfortunate Mister Renfield."

"It has been three days since Cromwell was admitted to my care. His behavior continues to bewilder me. He remains overjoyed by nearly everything; the confining nature of his chambers, the self-inflicted mutilation of his hand, the drugs I've administered to him, and the tasteless food we've forced him to consume! These things, which would try the patience of any sane man, make Cromwell happy!"

As he spoke, Seward once again began to browse through all the scraps of newspaper he had clipped from the daily pages over the last seventy-two hours.

"I wonder if it is my own paranoia, which has increased markedly since the strange affair with the Harkers, or if I might be correct when I seem to be detecting an unusual pattern in the recent newspapers. There seem to be a great number of people in London who are suddenly and inexplicably acting in very unusual ways. Cromwell is one example, but there are others, some in terrible ways, and some in more benign ways."

Seward completed his spoken diary entry just in time. A knocking sound came from the other side of his door. He called out for the knocker to enter.

Inspector Lestrade came shuffling in. He looked tired, unshaven, not well rested at all.

"Sorry to barge in, Doctor, but I had to know. Have you made any progress with that Cromwell bloke...the grinning one? I've scarcely been able to think of anything else since we brought him in."

Lestrade sat down in the chair by the desk, opposite Seward's chair and continued talking.

"I've seen some things in my time, I tell you, but this one's been keepin' me up all hours. Have you anything to tell me about him?"

Seward thought for a moment. He considered whether or not to tell Lestrade of his notice of the newspaper articles and his theory that there might be some connections present. He finally decided to speak his mind. The inspector couldn't arrest him for a theory.

"Inspector, I suspect there's more going on here than just Cromwell's state of mind...but I don't know how it all may be related. To be honest, I was thinking of sending for you. It seems you've saved me the messenger's tip!"

He picked up an assortment of the newspaper clippings from the desk, waving them at the Inspector, almost crushing them in his fist as he gestured.

"Have you been following the newspapers? Some of these incidents involve your department. People all over London seem to be suddenly acting in, shall we say, unexpected ways, much like our poor Mr. Cromwell. Now there's no obvious connection that I can see, but it makes me wonder, Inspector. It really makes me wonder."

Lestrade scratched his head. He seemed bewildered.

"So you can truly find no reason behind Cromwell's sudden madness?" the inspector asked. "No hint of a cause?"

Seward just shook his head, confirming that he indeed had no explanation.

"His peculiar happiness is genuine, so far as I can determine. He's been thoroughly examined. It's not drunkenness or syphilis or injury to the head. It's obviously not the dementia of old age as he's only thirty-seven. I see no noticeable defect that might cause such a thing, but I fear for the safety of all these others, if indeed it is a sort of pattern of unusual behavior that is emerging here in London!"

Seward's voice grew almost panicked as he thought more about the strange events as he spoke to Lestrade.

"And I can't seem to think of a way to determine if these fits of madness, if that is indeed what they are, are related. Is there any way, Inspector, that your department might look into this theoretical connection?"

Lestrade put down the newspaper clipping he had been glancing over. He shook his head.

"Doctor, my superiors would laugh in my face if I was to suggest such a thing, but I'll give you an idea. Were I in your position, I might think of consulting Mr. Sherlock Holmes."

Seward recognized the name.

"Holmes? Yes, I've heard the name," said the doctor, "but I've always thought his reputation to be somewhat exaggerated. He seems more of a character taken advantage of to sell sensational stories than a true investigator of matters as delicate as this one might be."

Lestrade's face grew deadly serious. He looked Seward straight in the eyes, like a man who wanted to make his point strongly and unmistakably.

"Oh no, Dr. Seward, though it wounds my pride to say so, Mr. Sherlock Holmes is the best you're likely to find at doing what it is that he does. If you truly believe in your suspicions in these matters, the only thing you should be doing now is speaking to him."

He picked up a scrap of paper and a pencil from Seward's desk and scrawled something across it.

"Here's where you're likely to find the man," he said as he handed the paper to Seward. "And Doctor, don't tell 'im I sent you."

Inspector Lestrade walked out of the office. Seward looked down at the paper in his hand to see what the police detective had written.

"221 B Baker St."

Seward put the address in his pocket. He left his office and went down to the level of the hospital where the patients were kept. He approached Abner Cromwell's cell and looked in through the little porthole in the door. There sat Cromwell on the bed. He was an average sized man with bushy brown hair and the stubble that resulted from several days without shaving. He was clad in the gray, pajama-like clothes typical of asylum patients. His right hand was wrapped in a rounded clump of bandages. The most striking thing about his appearance was the wide, wild grin on his face, far too happy for a man who was confined to a small cell with a grievous injury inflicted upon him. Seward shook his head at the sight of the man. He made up his mind. He would go to see this Holmes person immediately.

Within an hour, a hired cab had deposited Seward on Baker Street. He quickly found the correct building and walked up to the front door. He knocked.

Moments later, the door opened from the inside and Seward found himself facing a short, somewhat portly woman of about sixty.

"Can I help you, Sir?" she asked.

"Good day," said the doctor. "My name is John Seward. I'm looking for Mr. Sherlock Holmes. Would you perhaps be Mrs. Holmes?"

To Seward's surprise, the woman burst out laughing!

"Ha! Why I should hope not! I'm much too old for him…and far too sane! Why any woman in her proper mind would want to put up with that man's eccentricities is beyond my understanding! I'm Mrs. Hudson, the landlady."

She caught hold of herself and stopped laughing, looking slightly embarrassed about how she had reacted to Seward's question.

"I'm sorry, Sir, but Mr. Holmes is away," she said.

Seward was disappointed. Lestrade's confidence in Holmes' abilities had cemented the idea that his assistance was vital to Seward's quest for answers.

"I see," said Seward quietly. "Is there perhaps a way I might reach him? It is a matter of some delicacy and importance."

Mrs. Hudson shook her head and replied with a hint of sarcasm in her tone.

"Isn't it always that way with Mr. Holmes' visitors? I'm afraid I don't know where he's run off to, Sir…but perhaps you'd want to speak with Dr. Watson?"

Seward, unsure of who this Watson was, gave Mrs. Hudson a quizzical look.

"Dr. Watson?"

"The doctor is Mr. Holmes' friend and confidant," explained the landlady. "More often than not, if Mr. Holmes is off on some mysterious matter, Dr. Watson is right there along with him."

Seward agreed to meet this Dr. Watson fellow and followed Mrs. Hudson inside. She led him up a long staircase to the second story of the building. She knocked twice on a door and then pushed it open slightly and called out to the occupant inside.

"A Dr. Seward is here to see you, Sir!"

The door opened all the way and Seward walked in to see another man inside. He was a man of average height and weight, with full graying hair and a thick but neatly trimmed moustache. He was, at the least, a decade older than Seward. He was well dressed and Seward estimated him, on first impression, to be a man of fair intelligence and good manners.

Dr. Watson held out his hand in greeting.

"John Watson. What can I do for you, Sir?"

In another part of London, Jacob Morse stood atop the roof of the building in which he lived. He was a young man, still in his twenties, tall and slim with a clean-shaven face and wire-rimmed spectacles. Inside the building, where he kept a small apartment, Jacob Morse was just an ordinary young man with a menial job, but here, on the rooftop, he gazed down at the busy streets and felt like a king of all the small, ant-like, little people down below. He stood there, deep in thought, until the welcome voice of his new friend woke him from his contemplation.

"Good afternoon, Jacob."

Jacob Morse turned to greet his visitor. He smiled. He was faced with the sight of an unusual sort of creature, a demon! The thing that stood before him was a large, muscular thing, clad in a British Army jacket, with long, clawed fingers, a scowling face and two small horns protruding from its forehead. Jacob felt joy at the sight of the demon.

"Hello, Baalzephon!" he shouted.

Baalzephon looked directly at Jacob.

"So…when're you going to do it, lad? I think it's about time, don't you?"

"Do what?" Jacob asked.

Baalzephon's smile was replaced by a menacing glare, as if his patience with Jacob was wearing thin.

"Don't feign ignorance, boy! That dainty little thing selling flowers in the little shop down the road; you know what you want to do to her, don't you, boy? Don't you?"

Baalzephon's voice grew to a scream.

"Just take her! You and I are one and the same! You should know that by now! You are me and I am you! You are Baalzephon, captain of the guards of Hell! Start acting like it!"

Back at Baker Street, Watson and Seward had seated themselves in two chairs. After introducing themselves to each other, they had gotten down to business.

"And upon examining and interviewing Cromwell," said Seward, "I could discover no visible cause, either physical or otherwise, for his abrupt and self-destructive behavior."

Watson, who had been listening intently, replied.

"This Cromwell's actions are indeed mysterious and disturbing."

"Yes," continued Seward, "and after Cromwell's arrival at Carfax Asylum, I began to notice the sudden abundance of newspaper reports involving strange shifts in people's behaviors all around the city. From the violent outburst in the streets by an otherwise respectable banker…to the sudden emergence of Miss Clarice Bird as a musical talent of much note… to the inexplicable activities and bizarre emotional condition of our Mr. Cromwell…"

Watson interjected.

"Really, Doctor, self-mutilation and piano playing are hardly in the same category!"

Seward stood up. He wondered if Watson was beginning to doubt his sanity. Perhaps he had gone too far too quickly in bringing his suspicions to his fellow doctor's attention.

"I agree that I may be stretching credibility by seeing connections between these events," he said, "and I'll admit that some of my past experiences might lead me to be somewhat paranoid at times…which is why I sought out the advice of Mr. Holmes. I needed to voice my concerns to some intellect which I felt I could trust, and Mr. Holmes' reputation is quite widespread."

Watson gestured for Seward to sit back down.

"And a well-deserved reputation it is," he said, trying to calm Seward. "You were right to come here, although the absence of Holmes does present a problem. I see, Doctor, that you are sincere in your concerns, and so I will endeavor to help you. Perhaps I have learned something in all my years with Holmes. I shall try to put that experience to use."

John Seward felt a wave of relief wash over him. At least he would not be alone in what might very well turn out to be a wild goose chase.

"Thank you, Dr. Watson. Thank you. How do we begin?"

Watson stood and walked across the room to show Seward to the door.

"Come back here tomorrow morning," he said. "I wish to read all these news articles myself. The best thing to do would be to first learn of any connections between the subjects of all these stories."

With that, Seward left the apartment, proceeded to descend the staircase, and left 221 B Baker Street, content in the knowledge that he would be able to seek out answers to this most puzzling matter, and that he would not have to do it alone.

Chapter II:
An Open Book

Morning arrived in London. It was a bright, sunny day as Mary Harper took the key from her pocket, opened the door of the floral shop where she worked, and walked in. Mary did not own the shop; she was merely an employee, but it often came under her responsibility to be the one to open in the morning. She was only nineteen years of age, a slim, pretty young girl, not well-educated, but good at running the little shop. She wore typical working class clothes with a little apron tied in front. She set to work arranging flowers in the window display and tidying up the place for business.

As she dusted the countertop, she heard the small chime of the bell that hung above the door, indicating that the day's first customer was in the process of entering. She looked up to see Jacob, the young man from down the road, walking in. She smiled, having often thought that Jacob was quite handsome and hoping that he might someday become more than just a customer.

"Hello, Jacob," she said.

"Good morning, Mary," Jacob Morse replied, smiling too. He walked over to the counter as Mary came out from behind it to see if he needed help.

"Can I get you something?" she asked him.

Jacob's smile melted away and his face changed. Mary felt a bit of confusion as his face seemed to take on an aura of greed, lust, and a strange sort of exaggerated confidence.

"No, Mary. This time I've brought something for you!"

He rushed toward her. He grabbed onto the string of her apron and ripped it from her in one swift gesture. She looked shocked.

"Jacob, don't!"

He didn't listen. He grabbed hold of her and forced her behind the counter, out of sight of the window and anyone who might happen to glance in as they passed by. His hand muffled her screams and he did what he had come to do, all the while repeating to himself that he was indeed Baalzephon, captain of the guards of Hell.

Thirty minutes later, Jacob Morse walked away from the floral shop. He walked down the street, head held high, smiling and feeling like a king.

Behind the counter, Mary Harper sat trembling. Tears ran down her face, her dress was torn, and she could not stop whimpering.

John Seward rose early, dressed, and made a quick check of the condition of his patients, particularly Abner Cromwell. There had been no change. Cromwell's bewildering happiness continued and Seward wondered how long such a joyful mania could possibly continue before the patient came down from his clouds. In Seward's experience, such an extreme emotional state could not last forever. Eventually there would have to be a descent.

Seward left the asylum and made his way to Baker Street, anxious to learn what Dr. Watson had made of the newspaper articles that he had intended to read. Hopefully, Seward thought, Watson would agree that, theoretically at least, there might be some sort of connection between all those odd cases of behavioral shifts.

Seward knocked on the door, hoping that he was not intruding by calling so early in the day, but his fears were calmed when Mrs. Hudson promptly answered his knock.

"Good morning, Dr. Seward. Dr. Watson is waiting for you."

As he had on the previous day, Seward followed the landlady up the stairs and was admitted to the apartment that Watson shared with Sherlock Holmes. Seward sat down in the same chair he had occupied the day before, joining Watson, who was already seated. Not wanting to waste time with small talk, Seward got right to the point.

"I'm assuming you've read those articles, Watson. Have you reached a conclusion?"

Watson thought for a moment, considering how to phrase his reply.

"All of them were quite interesting when taken separately...but I still fail to see any connection between those persons involved."

Seward was disappointed.

"Behind the counter, Mary Harper sat trembling."

"I see," he said, despondently, but Watson reassured him.

"However, an opportunity for further investigation has presented itself."

He picked up a piece of paper from the table. From Seward's seat, it looked like an official letter of some sort.

"I've managed to arrange for us to visit Miss Clarice Bird," Watson revealed.

Seward was pleasantly surprised and suitably impressed.

"The suddenly emerging piano prodigy; how ever did you manage that, Watson?"

Watson laughed.

"Ha! You act as if it's such an extraordinary feat! Sherlock Holmes' brother, Mycroft, holds a position of some importance with Her Majesty's Intelligence Service. He arranged the meeting as a favour to me. Perhaps now we can discover a link between these seemingly unrelated events."

Seward was satisfied and encouraged. Perhaps now they could find some evidence that there was more to the apparent plague of insanity than the assumptions of his overly active imagination.

"It seems I made the right choice in coming to you then, Watson," he said.

By noon, Watson and Seward were on their way to the Bird residence. The cab dropped them off in front of the modest but well maintained house and they were admitted by Mr. Alexander Bird himself. Within minutes they were seated in the family's parlor. Mrs. Bird brought tea. Young Clarice came in and introductions were promptly made. Then the young woman sat down at the piano and began to play for her small audience of four.

Her fingers flew across the keys. Her parents, although they had heard her strange new sort of music before, could not prevent themselves from gasping in shock all over again, swept away by the eerie beauty of the notes. Seward was amazed by the unique quality of the music, but also kept a close watch on the girl's expressions and movements, always the psychiatrist, always on the job, always observing. Watson closed his eyes and listened, the majesty of the sound almost bringing a tear to his eye. He wondered what Sherlock Holmes, who had his own brand of unusual music, which he played on his violin while contemplating difficult cases, would think of Clarice Bird's performance.

When the long song had finally reached its conclusion, Clarice turned to those assembled and the trance-like expression she had acquired while playing melted away into an innocent smile.

"Was that satisfactory?" she asked the two doctors.

Both doctors broke into simultaneous applause.

"That was most extraordinary!" said Watson.

"Bravo! I have never heard music like that!" raved Seward.

The five occupants of the parlor sat down and had their tea. The Birds seemed like a normal, pleasant enough family to Watson and Seward. Everyone was quite polite to their guests and there seemed to be nothing unusual about Clarice Bird, other than her suddenly apparent musical talent, of course.

"Tell us, Miss Bird, how did you learn to play so beautifully?" Watson asked. "Your father has told us that you've never had a single music lesson, with the exception of one or two when you were a small child, which you disliked and promptly quit."

"That's correct, Sir," answered the young pianist.

Her dreamlike expression returned as she began her explanation in accordance with Watson's request. Seward immediately noticed the change in her facial features and watched with rapt attention.

"I was resting in bed one night, somewhere between being awake and being fully asleep," Clarice recalled, "when the oddest thing happened; I sneezed! And after I had sneezed…I could suddenly see the piano keys in my mind. At that moment, I knew those keys as if I had played them every day of my entire life…and all my lives past."

As she spoke, Seward analyzed every movement of her mouth and eyes, every bit of body language, and every hint from which he might gain some small insight into her state of mind. As he observed, he could not help but whisper one word to himself.

"Extraordinary."

The rest of the visit was rather uneventful. An hour later, the two investigators were on their way back to Watson's apartment. They had been deposited by their driver about a half mile from 221 Baker Street. They stopped for a meal and then walked the remaining way to their destination. As they walked, they discussed what they had seen at the Bird residence.

"As a medical doctor," said John Watson, "I can say that she appeared, at a glance, to be in perfect health. I saw no sign of distress or illness. What did you think of her state of mind?"

"She seemed happy," reported John Seward, "But there was something else. I'm not quite sure how to explain what I detected…but there was a very abnormal intensity to her when she was playing that music, as if …as if she became someone else for the duration of her song."

"It is indeed a fascinating case," said Watson as they reached the door of 221 B Baker Street. "I wonder what Holmes would make of it."

Mrs. Hudson opened the door as Watson reached for the knob, the kind of perfectly timed action that made him think she had been watching through the curtains for them to arrive, which indeed she had.

"Dr. Watson!" said the landlady with relief in her voice. "You're home! Oh, hello Dr. Seward. That Inspector Lestrade has been here waiting an hour for you, Sir. He's been upstairs pacing back and forth incessantly!"

"Lestrade?" said Watson, not having expected to hear that name. "What the devil does he want? Perhaps he doesn't know that Holmes is away."

"He may be looking for me," Seward chimed in. "It was Lestrade who suggested that I seek out Mr. Holmes, though he asked me not to tell you so."

The doctors made their way upstairs quickly and entered the apartment to find Lestrade standing there smoking a cigar.

"Hello, Inspector," said Watson. "I hadn't expected you to come by today."

Lestrade's face made the sly gesture that passed for his smile when he saw that both doctors had arrived together.

"Oh good, you've both come at the same time. Dr. Seward, I've brought you another one!"

"Another patient?" inquired the surprised Seward.

Lestrade produced his little notebook from his pocket, falling into his usual habit of pretending to consult his notes while repeating information that he had already memorized to perfection. It was a habit that was beginning to annoy Seward, who easily saw right through it.

"Jacob Morse, a twenty-six year old seller of artist's supplies," Lestrade began. "He's accused of suddenly criminally assaulting a young girl in the flower shop where she works. We'd have locked him up in our usual holding cells…but he kept claiming to be a "Citizen of Hell" or some other such gibberish, so I thought it a better idea to bring him to you. He's over at your place as we speak. I left him in the care of your man, Sullivan, just before coming here to find you. Sullivan said you had gone to see Dr. Watson this morning."

Seward did not hesitate a second. He turned and headed out the door. He had to get back to his hospital as soon as possible.

"Coming, Watson?"

At the Bird residence, Clarice had gone to her room once the two visitors had left. She needed some time alone. Outwardly, she had kept up an appearance of happiness, mostly to prevent her parents from worrying about her. In her mind though, she was terribly confused. She felt a sort of happiness when playing that piano, but it was not a normal happiness, for during those times Clarice Bird felt like she did not truly exist, like she were another person entirely. She sat on her bed and she fought off the urge to break down crying. What had happened to her simple life of just a week ago, she wondered? She had wanted nothing more than to complete her schooling, find the attention of a handsome suitor, or more than one, perhaps, and someday marry and have a family. Now though, the entire world seemed determined to transform her into a concert pianist. There were constant visitors coming to the house and she had to play for them all. She hadn't so much minded the two gentlemen who had come today; they were polite and seemed sincere and merely curious, which was understandable. It was all the others who made her uncomfortable; the men from the newspapers, the representatives from all those different orchestras and concert halls, and all sorts of others, all of whom wanted something from the Birds. Through all the commotion caused by her sudden ability to play that instrument, not a single person had asked Clarice Bird what she wanted to do with that ability.

The carriage raced through the streets. Watson had promised the driver an extra large gratuity if he made haste and got them to Seward's hospital as quickly as possible. The driver, encouraged by the pledge of higher pay, was doing his best to satisfy the doctor's request. As they travelled, the two doctors conferred.

"We'll both be seeing this one for the first time, Watson. It should be interesting to compare our initial observations afterwards."

"I agree, Seward. Depending upon our findings, perhaps we should go to see his unfortunate victim as well."

The driver made good and they soon disembarked in front of the asylum. They rushed inside. Seward's chief orderly, Sullivan, awaited them.

"Sullivan, where is he?" Seward asked excitedly. "Where is the new patient that Inspector Lestrade brought in?"

"Follow me, Sir!" Sullivan barked back as he turned to lead them down the corridor.

They had soon reached the cell into which Jacob Morse had been placed. Seward and Watson went inside while Sullivan stood guard outside. Morse was seated on the bed, his arms held fast by a straitjacket. He looked beat up, with bruises on his face, his hair disheveled, with traces of dried blood in some areas.

"Mr. Morse? Mr. Jacob Morse?" Seward said to him.

Morse's face grew into a defiant sneer.

"No, you're wrong! I am Baalzephon! Address me by my proper name from this moment forth!" he spat.

Watson went closer, examining Morse's beaten face.

"The constables seem to have mishandled him quite badly…but he's mostly just bruised. I don't detect any more serious injuries," the physician judged.

"Watson, look out!" shouted Seward!

Morse lunged forward, teeth bared, nearly biting Watson's face. Watson managed to jump backwards in the nick of time, narrowly avoiding injury.

The door swung open and Sullivan rushed in, grabbing hold of Morse and pinning him to the bed. Sullivan was a thickly built, strong man, and he had no trouble restraining the thin Morse, despite the animalistic fury which seemed to have driven him to try to assault Watson.

With Morse safely held down by the orderly, Seward shouted a question at him.

"Why, Mr. Morse? What made you assault that poor girl at the flower shop?"

Morse's face changed into a wild-eyed, malicious grin, his face gleaming with a confidence of disturbing quality as he hissed out his chilling answer to Seward's query.

"I take what I want. It is as simple as that. It is my right as captain of the infernal guards of Hell! There is no weak little Jacob Morse. I am Baalzephon! You mortals should be bowing before me now!"

Seward and Watson went to Seward's office to discuss matters after their intense encounter with Jacob Morse. Both took off their jackets and rolled up their sleeves. Watson took out his pipe, stuffed the bowl full of tobacco and lit it while Seward poured two drinks.

"Even I, without your psychological training," said Watson, "can clearly see that the man is insane."

"Doubtlessly," replied Seward, "but insanity may take any of many forms. The key to success in my profession is to be able to decide which."

Watson thought for a moment.

"In a change of behavior as drastic as the one we've just witnessed, there must be a cause, mustn't there, Seward?" Watson asked his companion.

"Certainly," the younger doctor replied, "although such causes can often be difficult to determine."

Watson considered something, unsure of whether he should suggest the idea, not knowing how Seward might respond. He finally decided to propose his idea and gauge Seward's reaction.

"Tell me, Seward, have you ever broken into someone's home?"

Seward's expression turned deadly serious as he answered.

"As a matter of fact, yes, I have."

Watson was shocked. He and Holmes had often had to resort to such stealthy tactics in the course of their investigations, but he could not imagine what occasion might lead a young doctor like Seward to go to such lengths and take such risks.

"You have; under what circumstances?" Watson asked curiously.

Seward's memory flashed back to the dark and terrible events of his past, specifically to the day when he and his companions had forcibly gained entrance to one of the houses being used by their foe, that Satan-spawned vampire, Count Dracula. He was certainly not going to relate that horrid adventure to Watson, so he gave a short, simple answer designed to, politely as possible, keep Watson from probing further into the matter.

"Under circumstances that I would much rather not recall…"

Watson could clearly see that he had touched a delicate nerve with his inquiry, so he went back to relating his plan.

"I see. I always carry my old service revolver of late, having been in some rather perilous scrapes while working with Holmes. Do you have a weapon?"

Seward produced a pistol from his desk drawer.

"All right, Seward. Let's go. We'll see if any light is shed on this mysterious matter by inspecting our patient's quarters."

The two doctors, both armed now, grabbed their coats and hats and left the hospital, both having grown to trust each other, neither hesitating to resort to even the illegal to seek out the answers to the questions that ran through both their minds.

It didn't take long for them to reach the building in which Jacob Morse lived. The address had been included with the information that Lestrade had provided for the hospital on Morse's admittance. It was a shabby looking building where the rooms were quite cheap. The front door was unlocked, as was often the case with the less desirable dwellings in that part of the city. Watson and Seward made their way up to the floor upon which Morse's room was located. They found the right door and Seward tried the knob.

"It's locked," he said. "How do we get in; break down the door?"

Watson smiled. He took out a small metal instrument and within seconds he had persuaded the lock to release itself and the door swung open with a soft creak.

"One does not keep company with Sherlock Holmes without acquiring a few useful skills," said Watson.

They entered the apartment. It was dark and dusty. Morse, being an unmarried young man, was obviously not much of a housekeeper. There was a single bed, unmade, heaps of clothing scattered on the floor, and a stack of a dozen or so books on the floor.

Seward began to dig through some of the clothing while Watson examined the books.

"There's not much here; just the belongings of a poor young student," said Seward. "Is there anything of interest among those books?"

Watson held up the volumes as he checked each one, not so much to show them to Seward as to take advantage of the daylight that was entering the gloomy room through the single window.

"*A History of the British Isles*, an issue of *The Strand*, Shelley, Poe, some very lurid novels…and this!"

Watson held up one particular book. It was a hardbound book, not very thick; perhaps one hundred and fifty pages, with a deep red cover and lettering in gold. Seward moved closer to Watson to get a better look at it.

"An odd-looking volume," Seward observed. "What is it?"

Watson read the title aloud.

"*The Book of the Howling Eyes*! This appears to be some sort of occult grimoire!"

He began to page through the book, pausing to take a longer look at certain pages.

"Yes," he said. "That's exactly what it is! This is a book of instructions for conjuring demons of all things! What utter rubbish!"

Seward took the book from Watson to examine it himself.

"Hmmm…an overly aggressive interest in such ideas could, theoretically, lead to Morse's mania. Still, this doesn't suggest any sort of connection to Cromwell, Miss Bird, or the others."

Seward continued to look through the book with Watson viewing it from over his shoulder. Seward opened it to the inside front cover and they both noticed something unusual. Inside the cover, there was a large tear, as if the endpaper was not fully glued down to the inner cover and had ripped. On the first actual page, facing the inner cover, some of the torn endpaper had stuck.

"This is strange…this tearing of the endpaper," Seward pointed out.

Watson held it up to the light and examined it more thoroughly.

"It was an error in the process of binding, I suppose."

Forgetting the apparent binding flaw for the time being, Seward continued to glance over the book's contents.

"I can certainly see how an obsession with this type of material could overwhelm the imagination of a young man. Perhaps our Mr. Morse is too easily taken to flights of fancy. Had he channeled that enthusiasm into poetry instead of rape he might have acquired a literary reputation!"

Watson took a small notebook from his pocket. He had also produced a pencil and was writing something down.

"I'm going to send a note to Lestrade. I want to see if he'll agree to send us any books that might have been found among Abner Cromwell's belongings."

Seward nodded, but expressed his doubts.

"I find it difficult to believe that two men might be similarly affected by a mere book, no matter how strange its contents."

"I concur," said Watson, "but we have nothing else to go on thus far."

The two doctors met next on the following morning. Watson arrived at Seward's hospital at quarter past nine and the two sat down to wait for the man they expected. Ten minutes later, Inspector Lestrade shuffled in, followed by a uniformed constable carrying a medium sized wooden crate.

"Morning, Gents," shouted the enthusiastic inspector. "As requested, here are Cromwell's books, though I don't see what a man's reading habits have to do with anything. Put it down on the desk, Constable."

"Thank you, Constable, Inspector," said Seward politely, but in a way that made it just clear enough that he would not be inviting the policemen to stay any longer. Lestrade got the message and left the office, taking his helper with him.

Seward sat behind his desk while Watson, who was standing, opened the crate and began to take the books out, one by one, announcing each one as he did so.

"A business ledger, *The Bible*, some Dickens…and here it is!"

He held up the copy of *The Book of the Howling Eyes* that had been in Cromwell's crate. Seward took it from Watson's hand.

"Perhaps there is a connection between the two men!"

Seward opened the book and was surprised to see the torn open endpaper inside the front cover and the piece of endpaper adhering to the first page, just as had been the case with Morse's copy of the same book!

"This one has the same tear in the inner front cover!" Seward pointed out excitedly. "Could the binding error have happened twice…or is this something more intentional?"

Both doctors looked through the book, each in turn. They both agreed that it was an exact duplicate of the one they had found in the quarters of Jacob Morse.

"We have both Cromwell and Morse here," said Seward. "We'll bring their books to them and observe their reactions."

Watson immediately agreed that Seward's idea was a good one.

"Yes," he said. "You take one to Cromwell, and I shall go to Morse."

Seward entered Abner Cromwell's cell with the book in hand. As he walked in the doorway, Cromwell jumped up from his seated position on the bed, grinning, overjoyed.

"You've brought it back to me! The doorway to infinite happiness! Oh my joy! Give it here, give it here!"

Seward handed the book to his patient, who grabbed it with his undamaged hand and held it to his face, sniffing it, inhaling deeply as if it smelled like the sweetest of perfumes.

"Oh thank you, my good doctor! Thank you!"

Watson walked into Jacob Morse's cell. Morse glanced up at his visitor. Seeing the book in Watson's hands, Morse's face became a twisted mask of greed and lust. Seeing Morse's expression, Watson was glad that the patient was still restrained by straitjacket.

"You have it, you dirty mortal," Morse hissed in a voice more demonic than human. "Baalzephon's book; it is mine! Mine, mine, mine! Get your hands off it, then!"

He lunged at Watson, teeth bared, as he had the day before.

"Mine!"

Watson, no weakling himself, and certainly no stranger to physically violent situations, dodged the onrushing maniac and let loose his fist, which connected in a punch to the wild man's jaw, sending him reeling back to land on the bed.

Watson tossed the book onto the bed and left the cell to see how Seward was faring with Cromwell.

Elsewhere in London, in the halls of a shadowy building, a tall thin man walked down the corridors, his face concealed by his hat and the collar of his coat, which was pulled up around his face. He stopped in front of the appropriate door and knocked three times.

The door opened just a fraction. The thin man could not see the face of the one who had opened the door, but could only hear the voice.

"It has come to my attention that the pattern of insanities has been noticed. We are being investigated…not by London's police, but by two private individuals."

The man in the hallway responded to the news.

"What would you have me do?"

A hand reached out from the opening in the doorway. It was an old-looking hand, with long, wrinkled fingers, long sharp nails, claw-like in their appearance. It held a package, a small parcel, wrapped in paper and tightly tied with string.

"Deliver this at once. The address is written on the package."

The tall, thin man left that building at once and made his way to the address on the mysterious package. Although curious, he never considered opening the package to examine the contents, not even for a second. He knew that such an act would be considered a betrayal, and he would not risk the potential penalty for such an act. He stopped at the front door of 221 Baker Street and gently knocked. A moment later, he was greeted by the sight of the plump, middle-aged woman who answered the door.

"Can I help you, Sir?" asked Mrs. Hudson.

"I have a package for a Dr. John Watson," said the thin man.

Mrs. Hudson smiled politely and took the package from the messenger. "He'll have it as soon as he returns."

Following their visits to Cromwell and Morse's cells, Seward and Watson returned to Seward's office to meet and discuss what they had each observed.

"So both subjects exhibited the same types of mania as earlier, with their reactions seeming to be quite intense when presented with the sight of that book," said Seward as he poured drinks for him and Watson.

"Agreed," Watson added. "Morse was loud and arrogant and again attempted violence. While Cromwell, as you related, was overcome by intense happiness yet again."

Seward began to jot down some notes as he continued the discussion.

"I find it remarkable that Cromwell has yet to express any remorse over his severed fingers, as if this onslaught of exaggerated joy dwarfs even such a grievous injury."

Watson yawned. It had been a long, eventful day and he was feeling tired. He stood and began to pull on his coat.

"It's gotten late, Seward. Will you call at Baker Street in the morning? We can discuss matters further and decide how next to proceed, over some of Mrs. Hudson's excellent coffee, of course."

Seward nodded and Watson left. It had grown dark by the time Watson reached his apartment. He left the carriage and went inside. Mrs. Hudson presented him with the package that had arrived earlier. He shrugged upon receiving it, not having been expecting a package of any sort. He ascended the stairs to his rooms; put the package down on the table, intending to open it before too long. He took off his coat and hat and sat down in the chair across from the fireplace. He sat back, formed his hands into a little triangle in front of his face as he had often seen Sherlock Holmes do when deep in thought, closed his eyes, and began to contemplate the bizarre behavior of Cromwell and Morse. His contemplation turned to drowsiness and he fell asleep where he sat.

Seward arrived bright and early the next morning. Mrs. Hudson let him in, smiling and cheerful. It seemed to Seward that Mrs. Hudson was always happy to see him. He suspected that this was due to the fact that he was, from what he had heard, more polite and much quieter than the man who usually spent most of the time there with Watson. Sherlock Holmes, from all that he had heard since becoming acquainted with Watson, Lestrade, and Mrs. Hudson, was a fascinating and brilliant, if somewhat eccentric man, and Seward hoped that he might someday meet the famous consulting detective.

After greeting Mrs. Hudson and inhaling the aroma of the coffee she had been brewing, Seward made his way up the steps and knocked on Watson's door. There was no response. He decided to see if it was unlocked. It was, so he simply entered. Watson was asleep in his chair.

"Morning, Watson," said Seward, hoping that the sound of his voice would be enough to rouse the sleeping physician from his slumber.

Watson opened his eyes, looking groggy and confused. He sat up and stretched.

"Morning...ugh...morning! I must have fallen asleep when I got home last night. It was a more tiring day than I had thought. Perhaps I'm getting old."

Seward laughed.

"Nonsense, Watson. Mrs. Hudson's magical coffee will rejuvenate you. What's that on the table?"

Watson glanced over at the table. He saw the package from the night before and remembered that he had not yet opened it. He picked it up and began to untie the string that held the paper on.

"This was left with Mrs. Hudson yesterday afternoon when I was with you and your patients. Let's see what it is."

He tore the paper off and gasped, holding up *The Book of the Howling Eyes*.

"Seward! It's yet another copy of that book!"

Seward walked over to get a closer look at the surprising contents of the package.

"This is fascinating! Who could have sent it, and why?"

"I don't know," admitted Watson as he began to open the book. "Let's see if it has that same odd damage to the endpaper..."

The cover swung open and there was a sudden sound of paper tearing as a cloud of thick white powder erupted forth, flying out of the book, right into the faces of Watson and Seward!

Chapter III:
Dust to Dust

The cloud of powder erupted all over the room, a burst of unexpected dust raining down after hitting Watson and Seward square in the faces.

"God Almighty!" shouted Watson.

Seward began to cough and choke on the dust that had entered his nose and mouth. Both men went into a moment-long panic, but quickly composed themselves as the powder began to settle, coming down out of the air to rest on the table and floor. Watson rushed to the window and flung it open to ventilate the room.

"Are you all right?" he asked Seward.

Seward gulped down a glass of water that had, fortunately, been left on the table. He put his hand to his head as if feeling a bit sick and trying to steady himself.

"I'm a bit dizzy," he said.

"We should get outside," said Watson.

The two hurried down the stairs and out onto the London street.

"At least now we know where the endpaper damage in all the books came from!" said Watson as they left the building. "Someone arranged it that way!"

"Brilliant in a malicious way," Seward opined. "Creating an envelope in the endpaper...and glued in such a way as to cause it to rupture upon one's opening of the book..."

They proceeded to stroll down the street, brushing remnants of the dust from their hair, faces and clothing as they walked.

"We'll walk until our heads clear," said Watson. "Are you feeling any better?"

"My head is still spinning a bit," Seward answered. "I seem worse off than you are. I must have inhaled more of that powder. What do you think it was?"

Watson could feel his own head starting to ache, but did not mention his discomfort to Seward.

"I don't know what it was, but it may be responsible for Cromwell and Morse's behavior. We'd best keep a close watch on each others' actions."

They walked another block. Seward had begun to sweat profusely. He staggered a bit and Watson helped him to steady himself.

"Why is this affecting me so much more, Watson?" Seward wondered out loud. "We were both hit with that sudden cloudburst."

"It's not just you, son," Watson responded. "I'm feeling it too. It's just the old Army stiff upper lip showing itself."

To Watson, though his head was spinning slightly and really aching now, the surroundings still looked the way he would have expected them to; people went about their daily business, horses pulled carriages by, and customers entered and exited shops. It was a typical London morning.

To Seward, however, things suddenly began to change. The buildings began to shift and stir, growing and changing into architectural oddities the likes of which he had never seen before. The people took on demonic qualities and the horses devolved into gruesome, dragon-like monstrosities. Seward began to scream out.

"What is happening? London...London has become a Hell!

Watson reacted immediately.

"Seward! Get a hold of yourself, Doctor! Calm down!" he said, grabbing Seward by the shoulders and looking into his panicked eyes. "What is it? What do you see?"

Seward stared back at Watson. His eyes were no longer those of a man with a firm grasp of reality.

"Hell on Earth! It's Hell on Earth!"

Watson looked Seward straight in the eyes and tried to talk him out of his sudden mania.

"Seward! John! You're a doctor! You can recognize a sick man! Look at yourself!"

Seward screamed back at him, shoving him away.

"Let me go! Don't let them get to us! Get back!"

Watson was pushed away and Seward began to run off into the streets. Watson was about to give chase when he heard a voice from behind him. It was a male voice, sounding middle-aged, with intelligence behind it, accented with an obvious tone of extreme sarcasm, taunting in its mean-spiritedness.

"Feeling lost without your smarter friend, are you, Johnny Boy? Holmes would have the whole thing under control by now, wouldn't he? He'd have none of this running around like madmen in the streets! Reason, logic, deduction! Those are the keys, Johnny! You should know that by now!"

Watson turned around and found himself face to face with the one man whom he had always dreaded more than any other. It was a man whom Watson had never seen in person, but he knew him immediately. The face he saw before him matched the image in his mind's eye, created mostly by Holmes' description, perfectly.

"You!" shouted Watson. "Moriarty...of course it's you! But...but..."

Watson could feel the sweat beginning to trickle down his face. He was feeling worse, losing his grip. He knew he was falling into the same state that had caused Seward to run off into the streets.

"No! It can't be you! You're dead," Watson said to the man who he now faced. "You went over the falls, smashed to bits on the rocks! You are not real!"

Before Watson's eyes, the face of Moriarty began to melt, to change, to shift forms.

"Yes!" Moriarty hissed, in a voice that was suddenly serpentine. "I am dead!"

Moriarty was gone, replaced by a normal-looking man, a startled stranger.

"Why are you addressing me in such a manner?" the gentleman demanded of Watson. "Do I know you? Are you ill?"

Watson, suddenly aware that he had been speaking to an innocent man who his feverish mind had molded into an old enemy, could only mutter his apologies.

"I'm...I'm sorry," he said quietly, feeling ashamed and hurried past the man, knowing he had to find Seward quickly.

Seward ran. He dodged the people who looked like demons to him and just kept going. He could not think, but only felt panic, fear, and confusion.

He ran with his eyes wide, his mouth agape, his mind a clouded mess of sheer terror.

He turned down a narrow alleyway between two buildings. He was alone. No demons had followed him. He could pause, rest for just a moment, and try to gather his fleeting thoughts. He fell to his knees. He was not a religious man, but the genuflection was instinctive, some long grown out of childhood habit coming back in a moment of mental crisis. He did not beg some deity for guidance though, but began to talk to himself, as if searching for the intellect and reason that he knew was still within, beneath the layers of insanity with which he was now faced.

"Sane…stay sane, Doctor…or you'll wind up in a cell with Renfield! No. Wait. He's dead. Renfield is dead…long dead. He's long dead and buried."

Seward heard a sound above him, a familiar sound, the noise of something moving, hovering, like the steady beat of wings. A shudder went through him. He looked up from where he knelt. As he did, his face went paler than it had been a moment before. His fear grew even deeper.

"You!" he shouted.

Above him hovered a strange, certainly not human, monstrous thing. The body was roughly human in shape, but not quite. It was a grotesque parody of humanity, covered in thick, coarse hair, possessing wings which beat slowly but steadily, keeping it aloft just high enough to look down upon the helpless Seward. The thing's face was familiar, too familiar, to John Seward. It was the face of Dracula, the foul undead thing that had turned Seward's life, and that of his dearest friends, and his poor Lucy, into a living nightmare. They had, or so Seward thought, destroyed the vampire, but not before it had taken Lucy forever, and killed Quincy Morris at the sight of their final battle. Now, many months later, Seward again looked into the undead eyes of Dracula, and the part of him that was best equipped to recognize a hallucination was lost for the moment, mired in the depths of lunacy!

"Frightened little physician," said Dracula, "did you really think your friends and your mentor had done away with me permanently? Did you truly think an immortal could so easily fall? I live! I live! I shall always live!"

The vampire descended a bit closer to ground level, to Seward, his undead mouth opening, fangs bared, already dripping with blood.

Watson was still walking along the streets. He was still half dazed, but was struggling mightily to keep his senses from misleading him again. He

"The vampire descended...its undead mouth opening..."

had to find Seward; he knew the poor young man had been more greatly affected by the strange dust they had both been exposed to.

As he walked, he could tell that his vision was growing cloudy and his head beginning to spin. He hoped he could hold on to his senses, but he feared for his own sanity as well as that of Seward. Perhaps the phantom of Moriarty had been right, he thought. Perhaps he was not equipped to handle a situation like this alone. Perhaps he needed Holmes. He stopped in his tracks and found himself mired in doubt.

"Dr. Watson, Dr. Watson!" shouted a voice from behind him.

He felt a strong hand come down upon his shoulder, and he felt himself pulled around, whirled to face the owner of that hand.

"Are you well, Doctor?"

The face that Watson saw was a blur to him; a blur of nose and mouth and two dark eyes and bushy sideburns, but it would not come into focus clearly enough to be identified. Was it friend or foe? Watson could not take any chances now; he had to treat the face and the hand as potential enemies.

"Unhand me, you malicious devil! I'll strike you down where you stand!" Watson threatened.

Watson's threat did little good, for he found himself in a headlock, the victim of a quick maneuver, backed by great strength.

"Easy now, Doctor, you'll feel better in a moment," said Sullivan, the chief orderly at Seward's hospital. He forced Watson's head back at an angle and poured the liquid contents of a small vial into the doctor's mouth.

Watson swallowed involuntarily. He couldn't help himself. He felt the liquid, which possessed an almost sickening sweetness with a definite chemical taste, slide down his throat. He coughed several times, and his vision suddenly began to clear. He watched with amazement as the mass of hair and skin that had just accosted him began to take the shape of Seward's assistant.

"Ugh..." groaned Watson. "Sullivan?"

The bulky orderly nodded.

Seward stared up at Dracula. He forced himself to speak, despite his almost overwhelming horror at the sight of his old foe.

"You're dead! We destroyed you, you unclean, unholy thing! Poor Quincy gave his life so you would haunt humanity no more!"

The bat-winged abomination came even closer to the terrified doctor.

"You are so very, very wrong, my dear little doctor. I live! And I hunger once more for blood!"

Seward fell backwards from his kneeling position, crawling in reverse, inching back, desperately trying to escape the bared fangs of the vampire lord.

"No! Get back to Hell where you belong!"

He pulled his pistol from his pocket, aiming it at the thing that hovered just above him. His finger tensed on the trigger.

"Get away from me! Get back!"

Watson sat on the cobblestone ground looking up at his unexpected savior, Sullivan. His head was beginning to clear, but he was still not feeling normal or in full control of his senses.

"How do you feel, Dr. Watson?" Sullivan asked.

"A bit dizzy, but much better; I think I'm starting to be able to distinguish reality from hallucination again. What was that foul tasting liquid that you forced down my throat?"

Sullivan helped the shaky Watson to stand up as he explained.

"It's a mixture that Dr. Seward developed. We often give it to patients when hallucinations begin. It seems to help in some cases, although we can never seem to predict precisely when it will help and when it will make matters worse."

Watson was able to stand on his own now. He stretched, as if he were waking up from an afternoon nap.

"Did you try to use it on Morse and Cromwell?"

"No," answered Sullivan. "It has to be given at the start of hallucinations. Otherwise, it may as well be water. Luckily, I found you soon enough."

Watson nodded.

"What are you doing here anyway? Tell me as we walk. We have to find Seward; he was worse off than I was."

They began to walk down the streets, unsure of how to begin trying to locate Seward.

"I thought Dr. Seward would be with you," Sullivan explained, "so I came down to Baker Street to tell you both...Abner Cromwell is dead!"

Watson was surprised to hear the news.

"How?" he asked.

"It seems he came out of his strange haze of happiness," Sullivan said. "He realized he'd lost his sense of reason, I suppose. He saw what he had done to his hand...and decided to bash his head against the wall...over and over again...until he'd split his skull open! He was a bloody mess when I found him!"

The two men continued to walk, minutes passing by with no sign of Seward's whereabouts. Then a sudden loud cracking sound came in the distance.

"A gunshot!" said Sullivan.

Watson began to run. Sullivan followed.

"Seward may have had his revolver with him!" shouted Watson as they moved. "Let's go!"

They ran in the direction from which the shot had come.

"I hope you have more of that concoction you just made me drink!" said Watson.

"Of course I do!" Sullivan confirmed. "I always carry several doses on my person."

They heard a second shot and turned left, down the alley from which the shot seemed to have come. There was Seward, about fifty feet ahead of them, waving his revolver in the air and shouting madly.

"Back to your grave, demon!" he shouted, his face a mask of panic and shock.

"Why won't you die?"

Watson and Sullivan approached as quickly as they could.

"Seward, put down the revolver!" Watson cried out.

The order only served to make matters worse, as Seward turned his gaze from whatever he thought he was seeing, to the very real figures of Watson and Sullivan.

"More devils! Back, back, or I'll shoot!"

Watson and Sullivan kept coming, praying they would reach Seward before the trigger could be pulled again. He fired! Luckily, his aim was distorted by his mania and the bullet struck no one.

"Thank God! He missed!" Watson shouted in relief.

Sullivan reached Seward first, plowing into him and pinning him to the ground. Seward struggled, but he was not nearly as strong as the stout Sullivan.

"In my right pocket, Doctor, get the vial!"

Watson took the vial of liquid from Sullivan's pocket and poured it into Seward's mouth as Sullivan held him down. Seward swallowed, although some of the substance did trickle down his chin. His eyes rolled back in his head and he collapsed into unconsciousness. Sullivan lifted the thin doctor and tossed him over his shoulder like a life-sized rag doll.

"Back to my apartment, Sullivan," said Watson.

They reached Watson's apartment without further incident. Sullivan deposited Seward on the couch and Watson placed a wet cloth on his forehead. He seemed to be all right; breathing normally and apparently just asleep. Watson would keep watch over him until he awoke, and Sullivan also refused to leave. Watson was pleased to see that Mrs. Hudson had taken it upon herself to clean up the powder that had been launched from the endpaper of the book.

"That's a fine, brave landlady you have there," said Sullivan, "cleaning up that foul powder for you."

"As long as she took care not to breathe it in," replied Watson, "she was fine. It settled once the initial burst from the book was done."

On the couch, Seward groaned a bit, waking up. His eyes opened and he gave a half-hearted smile.

"How do you feel?" Watson asked.

Seward sat halfway up, testing his strength.

"Better, much better. When I created that anti-hallucinatory solution, I never thought I'd be ingesting it myself one day. In my half-asleep state, I heard the two of you talking. It's a shame about Cromwell. I had hoped to help him out of his fog. Perhaps there's still some hope for Jacob Morse."

Watson nodded in agreement.

"We now know how Morse and Cromwell reached their strange states of behavior," he said, "but I find myself wondering how Miss Bird was exposed to that powder...and why its effects seem only to have benefited her rather than induce such mania as the two men were overcome by."

Seward sat up all the way now. He swung his legs off the couch and planted his feet on the floor. He stood, a bit shaky, but all right.

"Then I suggest we pay a visit to the Bird residence tomorrow," he said. "We'll bring along our copy of that book, provided we can get all of that infernal dust out of it. Come, Sullivan, back to the hospital. I need to rest before our excursion tomorrow. I'll return in the morning, Watson."

Chapter IV:
Ghosts of the Past and Present

Many hours later, Bess Fletcher walked along Osborn Street in the area of London known as Whitechapel. She was tired, she was hungry, but she could not stop for the night yet. She needed a little more money; just a job or two more and she'd have enough for the night's work. Bess Fletcher was twenty-six years old, but looked a few years older, as life on the streets of Whitechapel was not easy. She was no beauty, but wasn't entirely homely either. At least she was attractive enough, despite malnourishment and some missing teeth, to attract a decent number of clients. Of course, most men who frequented the streets of the area for pleasure were not the finicky kind. The streets were dark so late at night, but Bess was used to it.

It had just begun to rain lightly, enough to annoy, but not enough to soak, when she saw a man walking towards her. She stopped and waited for him to reach her, hoping he would stop. He did. He was a middle-aged man, well dressed; better dressed than most men who walked those streets at that time of the night. A few words were exchanged. A bargain was struck. Bess Fletcher and her client, hopefully the last of the night, went down an alley to a small, secluded spot behind a building, out of sight of passersby and policemen. Bess lifted her skirt. As she did so, she saw the flash of the pale, cloud-blurred moonlight reflecting off something shiny and steel. She didn't see anything else after that.

Minutes later, the client wiped the crimson from his blade and concealed the weapon in his coat. He calmly walked back out onto Osborn

Street and was on his way. As he walked, he smiled. It felt good to be back in action. He had been away for far too long.

Inspector Lestrade literally had to shove his way through the crowd of newspaper men on the steps of Scotland Yard when he arrived in the morning. They all seemed to be shouting at once, with such fervor that he could hardly hear what they were all saying. Wondering what had them so excited and demanding attention, he pushed through the mob and went inside.

"What in God's name is that ruckus about outside?" he asked the first person he saw, a young detective named Long.

"You'd better go and ask the commissioner, Inspector. He wants to see each of the senior inspectors as soon as they arrive. He's returned, Sir, and once the public hears, I don't know how we'll keep them from rioting in the streets!"

Lestrade was confused.

"Who, Long? Who's returned? What are you talking about?"

Watson woke early, and was surprised to find that he felt fine. He was well rested, a bit hungry, but his head was clear, nothing hurt, and the nightmarish ordeal of the previous day was just a memory now. He could smell breakfast cooking downstairs and thanked whatever powers might govern the universe for the quality of Mrs. Hudson's cooking. He made his way to the sitting room and went to the window. It was a bit stuffy inside and he wanted to let some air in. He opened the window and was surprised by the amount of noise outside. Baker Street was usually fairly busy, but the buzz of myriad conversations was much louder than usual for so early in the day.

Mrs. Hudson entered with a tray of food and tea. She put it down on the table.

"Good morning, Dr. Watson," she said.

"Mrs. Hudson," Watson asked her, "have you been outside yet today? What on Earth is all that noise? Why are the people so excited?"

"Oh, Doctor, it's terrible!" she said, and Watson was surprised to see the normally unflappable landlady so flustered. "There's been a murder, Sir. But it's not just a murder. One of the working girls out in Whitechapel, Sir, she was done in just like the others, all the others from before. They say it's Old Jack come back to start all over again!"

Watson did his best to calm poor Mrs. Hudson, telling her it was too soon to jump to conclusions, as the people outside apparently had, and sent her downstairs after thanking her for the breakfast. He always made an effort to thank her, since he knew that Holmes often neglected to do so.

He sat and began to eat. He knew that the lives of London's prostitutes were hard ones and they did sometimes meet violent ends. He knew that the public could sometimes jump to conclusions when such news became public knowledge. Furthermore, he knew certain things that made it plain to him that the rumors could not possibly be true. He put the matter out of his mind and finished his breakfast while he waited for Seward to arrive.

An hour later, Seward arrived. Watson poured two cups of tea as the younger doctor sat down.

"I apologize for being late, Watson," said Seward. "Lestrade came by this morning to get the details of Cromwell's suicide for his report."

"Lestrade?" said Watson. "Did the good inspector have anything to say about this murder that has the public so abuzz today?"

"He did," Seward answered. "He was quite shaken by it. It seems that a Whitechapel woman called Fletcher was killed last night in a very grisly manner; disemboweled and otherwise mutilated. The whole police department is scrambling to look for clues. The public is going to panic, if they haven't done so already. Lestrade even seemed half-convinced that it's Jack the Ripper himself, come back and ready to go on a spree like he did before. I don't understand it. Why would he resurface after a decade? Where did he go and why return now?"

Watson was silent for a moment. He considered how to phrase what he was going to say next. He wanted to tell Seward something, and he had certainly come to trust him over the past few days, but he knew that he could not reveal too much.

"My thoughts have been flowing in a different direction since I heard the rumors this morning," he began. "I keep wondering if this murder, apparently in imitation of The Ripper, might not be another case of the rampant insanity that we've been investigating. After all, we don't know how many copies of that infernal book exist, and to whom they were distributed."

"But Watson," Seward interjected, "what if it really is Jack the Ripper?"

Watson laughed a little. It was not that he found the situation humorous, but he wanted to lighten the heavy tone of the conversation just enough to soothe Seward's concern a bit.

"My boy, it couldn't possible have been the real Jack the Ripper who killed that poor girl last night," he told Seward.

"And how the devil would you know that?" Seward asked.

Watson's answer stunned Seward to the point that he almost spilled his tea.

"Because he's dead…and it was I who killed him."

Seward could not take another sip; for fear that he would choke on it.

"What?" he said, astonished by Watson's statement. "Tell me more!"

Watson paused to pour more tea into his cup, and then began to speak again.

"I'll tell you what I can, but I'm afraid it may leave you with more questions that I cannot answer. When the Ripper murders occurred in the autumn of '88, it was inevitable, given the brutality and prominence of the crimes, that Sherlock Holmes would become involved. I, of course, went along with him. It did not take too long for the sheer power of his intellect to deduce the identity of the murderer. I only wish that he had joined the chase sooner, for that may have spared the lives of some of the victims. Once we had ascertained the Ripper's identity, we went to apprehend the fiend. We found his residence, which was a rather large house. Inside, we became separated. Holmes found our target first and the two became locked in a physical struggle. When I reached them, the killer, who's maniacal fury made him stronger than a normal man, had Holmes at a disadvantage and was about to plunge a surgical knife into his throat. I, acting in the only way that seemed possible given my position in relation to the scene, threw an oil lamp at the killer. He burst into flames. Holmes was able to move out of the way of the fire and remain uninjured. Jack the Ripper, as he has been known ever since, burned to death before my eyes. Only the highest officials of the Crown and the police force were privy to the knowledge that the murderer was found and killed. His identity was one that it was not deemed wise to reveal publicly. Holmes and I were made to swear an oath, before Her Majesty, that we would never divulge his name under any circumstances. That, my friend Seward, is all that I am at liberty to tell you. I do hope that you understand."

Seward smiled.

"There ought to be a statue of you in a prominent place in London!" he said. "It is an honor and a privilege to know you, Dr. Watson!"

Watson chuckled.

"Don't make so much of it, Seward. It was only one of many dangerous situations I have faced with Holmes, and I acted purely out of concern for his well being."

They finished their tea and politely declined Mrs. Hudson's offer to bring a fresh pot. When the landlady had cleared away the cups and the remains of Watson's breakfast, and had left the room again, Watson stood and glanced at the clock.

"Well Seward, I suppose its late enough now to make our way to the home of Clarice Bird and her parents. We can look into this pseudo-Ripper business later."

The two doctors left the building, hailed a hansom cab, and were on their way.

They arrived at the Bird residence at around noon. They left the cab and went up the front walkway to the door. Watson had brought his black doctor's satchel with him; he did not want *The Book of the Howling Eyes* to be visible, at least not yet. Though unexpected, they were greeted warmly by Mrs. Bird, who admitted them to the house and apologized for the fact that Clarice was not home, as she had gone to have lunch with a friend. Watson told her that it was all right and, if possible, they would like to speak with Mr. Bird.

She led Watson and Seward down the house's hallway to Alexander Bird's study and let them in. The Bird family patriarch was seated behind his desk. He greeted them warmly, invited them to sit down. They each took to one of the two chairs that were placed in front of Bird's desk. Once they were comfortably seated, Mrs. Bird left the room and closed the door behind her.

"How is your daughter, Clarice, Mr. Bird?" Watson asked to begin the conversation.

"The same, I suppose," was the answer from Alexander Bird. "She seems happy enough; plays that piano almost constantly."

Having given the answer that Watson had expected to hear, Bird took on a different facial expression. His brow wrinkled with apparent worry and he went on.

"Honestly, doctors, perhaps she seems to be a bit too obsessed with the damned thing. On some nights the music goes on and on for all hours. It's a miracle that her mother and I managed to talk her into going out today."

Seward, who so far had said nothing, simply watched as Bird spoke. He was carefully observing Bird's facial expressions, using his skills as a psychiatrist. Watson reached down into his doctor's bag, which lay on the floor next to his chair. He took out the book he had brought with him and held it up for Alexander Bird to see.

"Tell me something, Mr. Bird. Are you familiar with this book?"

Bird jumped up from his chair, nearly knocking the piece of furniture over in the process. He had suddenly become very excited, shocked by the sight of that book.

"Where did you get that?" he demanded to know.

Seward interjected his own question into the conversation.

"So you have seen it before? Do you possess a copy of it yourself?"

Bird reached into his desk drawer and took out his own copy of the book. He waved it in front of Seward and Watson excitedly.

"I certainly do! It's right here. But the two of you should have no idea that it even exists. You haven't earned the right!"

His outburst over, Bird sat back down and busied his hands straightening his collar, a motion which Seward judged to be an effort to compose himself, calm his temper, which had just demonstrated its capacity to flare up suddenly.

Bird's reaction to seeing the book had aroused Watson's curiosity, and he was especially intrigued by the last part of Bird's loud statement.

"We haven't earned the right?" Watson asked. "Well someone thinks we did! This copy of the book was delivered to my residence…and almost drove Dr. Seward and myself into an abyss of insanity! You owe us both an honest explanation!"

Seward reached across the desk and picked up Bird's copy of the book. "Let me see that."

He opened the cover and looked inside. The same tearing of the endpaper as had been found in the other three copies was evident in this one as well.

"It's been opened, and the dust released," Seward pointed out. "Did you open this book, Mr. Bird? You don't seem to be under the same effects as certain others."

Bird leaned back in his chair. He suddenly looked tired and it was becoming obvious to Seward and Watson that he did not want to speak about the book or any subjects related to it.

"I was not permanently affected because I knew how to control my reactions to the powers of this book," he said, "and the substance used to enhance those powers. My daughter, however, was not sufficiently prepared for the divine experience."

Watson was outraged by Bird's last phrase. He leaned forward in his chair, glaring straight into Bird's eyes.

"You deliberately exposed a mere child to that powder, that drug? What kind of a father are you?"

Bird argued back at him, defending himself.

"I didn't do it intentionally! The powder was on my desk. Clarice came in to say 'goodnight.' I put some papers on the desk to conceal the powder from her notice, but she must have inadvertently inhaled some of it. I didn't mean for it to happen! I was just relieved, more relieved than you know, that the result turned out to be a blossoming of musical talent and not something more malignant. I've been following the papers. I know what's become of some of the others."

Seward stood and looked down at Bird. He was angry now, thinking of his two patients, Cromwell and Morse, and ready to say or do anything to get Bird to reveal anything he knew about the circumstances surrounding the whole chain of events.

"Mr. Bird, you owe us an explanation! Tell us everything you know about this book, this powder, this whole affair!"

Seward sat back down, and Bird stood again. Watson's muscles tensed, as he prepared to move if Bird should try to strike Seward or flee the room, but no action would be necessary; Bird looked calm now and he smiled, though it was a weary smile.

"I'll pour us some drinks, gentlemen," said Bird, "and I'll relate my story."

A moment later, Watson and Seward each had a drink in hand and they sat back in their chairs awaiting Bird's tale. Bird, who had taken his seat again after pouring the drinks, leaned forward in his chair, leaning his arms on his desk and looked straight at his two companions.

"I hardly know where to begin, but I suppose a bit of background might be in order. I judge you both to be men of fair intelligence and I find it likely that either of you would agree that the lust for power has always been one of the most prominent characteristics of human behavior. I'm sure you have both known men whose lust for power...and perhaps even for ultimate knowledge and immortality have driven them to great lengths to attain their desires."

As Bird spoke of such men; those who would go to any lengths to gain their ultimate goals, Watson and Seward could not help but see, in their minds' eyes, the men who, for them, exemplified that type of action more than any others; Watson saw the face, as he imagined it to be, of Professor Moriarty, and Seward could vividly see the fanged countenance of Dracula staring at him out of the darkness of the past.

"And so," Alexander Bird continued, "I will begin my tale on the subject of the great lust that has driven many men to such unorthodox actions."

Bird thought back to his childhood as he spoke. He recalled the days of his youth and his upbringing. He remembered attending church with his parents and how the stern-faced minister delivered his sermons with such zeal that it nearly scared him out of his wits when he was a small, impressionable boy.

"Like all young boys of my age and nationality I was, at a young age, indoctrinated into the religion of my parents…and their parents before them. I went to church with my parents as a child, mostly because I had no choice. I was their son and I did as I was told to do. The words of the church's leaders seemed to satisfy, to comfort, and to reassure most of the adults I knew then…but it didn't lull me into any sense of satisfaction; it was just the opposite. I found myself unable to accept answers simply because I was told that they represented the truth about the world, about mankind, and about God. From an early age, I wondered about things and often wished I could learn more; see beyond the things that were taught to me by those who took responsibility for my upbringing."

"Years passed and I fell into the same patterns of life as my contemporaries. I attended the university, gained the standard education of those in my place and time. I fell in line with societal expectations. I took a wife, lived life as my father had done before me. I had a profession and a family. And there I sat, a mature London gentleman with a house, a daughter, plenty of money…and still that lack of satisfaction crept back to the forefront of my thoughts!"

"Over the years, I had heard mentions of those who gathered in secret, or at least in semi-secret, learning about schools of thought and fountains of knowledge that were not part of the standard religious and academic experience of the typical citizens of Britain. I became a Freemason. I was inducted into that brotherhood and quickly worked my way up through their ranks, hoping to become privy to some information that would satisfy my intellectual and spiritual needs…but I soon found their strict initiations and pompous ideas to be lacking the power and mystery I sought."

"Then one day, one of my fellow Masons gave me some intriguing information. It seemed that there were a group of men who had devoted themselves to searching more deeply for the things that lie beyond the boundaries of common belief. He gave me a card on which was written the name *Navigators of the Inner Planes*. With the name was a dramatic symbol; the image of an eye with a sword going straight through it."

"I followed the instructions I had been given for making contact with that group of men. I soon acquired an address and made my way to the appropriate part of the city, where I knocked upon the door with the correct number. I found what I wanted and was welcomed into one of their meetings."

"There were five of us present at the first meeting. We found ourselves seated in a mostly dark room. None of us knew what to expect next, so we talked amongst ourselves as we waited for something to happen. We introduced ourselves to each other. There was myself, young Jacob Morse, who seemed somewhat shy, but enthusiastic, Abner Cromwell, who seemed somewhat dimwitted, which made me wonder why he was there, a banker named Edwin Cooper, whom you may recall from last week's newspaper article about the man who rampaged his way through a crowded street and nearly beat two policemen senseless, and a fifth man, who refused to tell us his last name, introducing himself only as Terence. As we talked, we all seemed to agree on one thing; that we all wished to know more than what we already knew, that we all sought a different point of view."

"We sat together for nearly an hour, wondering if anything else was to occur. Finally, our host entered the room, from a doorway to the side of the room that we had not even noticed. He was a man of average height and weight, dressed in a long robe. When he entered the room, his face was concealed by a hood which was drawn up around his head, casting shadows on his face. He drew back the hood and we could see him. It was difficult to judge his age, but I would estimate that he was between forty and fifty years. He was bald, completely, as if he shaved his head daily. What struck me most vividly was that he possessed the most piercing, intense pair of eyes that I had ever seen. The pupils were of an almost pure black, giving the impression that he was most certainly not the type of man whom one would want to have as an enemy. He refused to tell us his name, but the sheer weight of his presence, the intensity in his eyes, assured us that we were indeed in the company of a rather unique man."

"He never sat down with us, but moved about the room, looking at each of us in turn as he spoke. I recall his words almost exactly. He told us that many ancient books, the texts of many religions, most of the sources from which we have culled our various mythologies, have spoken of demons! He asked if any of us knew exactly what a demon was. It was young Jacob Morse who spoke up first. He sounded nervous in the presence of the Hooded Man, but he tried to participate in the discussion. According to myth, he said, demons are evil spirits, fallen angels placed in Hell to torment the souls of the damned. Once Morse had offered his answer to the question, the Hooded Man leaned in close to him, with the manner of one who is about to reveal a grave secret. He spoke directly to Morse, but loudly enough that we could all hear him. 'Yes, Mr. Morse,' he said. 'That is indeed one interpretation of what a demon is, but there are other ideas related to that word, ideas which I will share with you tonight!' That statement piqued all our interests, and we began to listen intently to everything that the Hooded Man began to tell us."

"He turned his attention from Morse's face to a position that allowed him to look at all of us simultaneously. 'Our young friend Jacob,' he said, 'was quite correct in his answer, but I would like to speak of a different interpretation of the idea of demons. This one, in my humble opinion, is far, far more interesting. The word demon originated with the Greek word daimon, which meant a genius or a spirit. Looking at the word and what it represents, from a different angle, we might decide that perhaps it means something other than what it is usually thought of as being in present day religious connotations. Perhaps it will make sense to you, my friends, if we think of demons as representing parts of the human mind. There are many impulses which control us, of which we are often not even aware. These wild spirits within us often exert an immense degree of control over our actions...when in fact it should be we who control them! By visualizing our inner demons as actual beings, as separate entities from ourselves, we can rule over them and subordinate them to our wishes! We can then control ourselves...and grant ourselves absolute power over all we need and all we desire!' The Hooded Man paused then, perhaps thinking that it would be a good idea to give us an opportunity to digest the ideas he had just revealed to us. I cannot speak for the others, but I was intrigued."

Bird stopped talking for a moment and looked at Watson and Seward. He took a sip of his drink and then spoke once more.

"Gentlemen, has all of what I have said thus far been clear to you?"

Watson nodded and Seward spoke.

"Yes, Mr. Bird," he said. "It has been perfectly clear. As a doctor of the human mind, I find the symbolism of the idea to be quite interesting."

Satisfied that his guests had thus far been able to follow his tale, Alexander Bird continued his narrative.

"That meeting was the first of several. The Hooded Man later taught us certain exercises meant to enable us to control our minds, first through control of our bodies and breathing, and later by means of stopping distracting thoughts as they arose in the mind. I, for one, felt that I was doing quite well in following the teachings of our mysterious and nameless mentor. I was not sure how deeply the others understood what we were being taught. Jacob Morse was quiet and so it was difficult to gauge his progress. Cromwell, as I stated earlier, seemed, to put it mildly, quite a stupid man, so I doubt if he had much comprehension of the things the Hooded Man said to us. Cooper and Terence seemed to understand the instructions they were given, but I cannot say for certain how deeply that understanding went. I really had no strong opinions about Edwin Cooper. He seemed to be a man of average intelligence, polite and quite normal, with no distinguishing characteristics to his personality. The one called Terence, on the other hand, struck me as a bit too intense of a man, with a strange hostility seething beneath the surface of his personality; he was the kind of man who, it seemed to me, could easily lose control of his self-control and give in to destructive impulses. Of course, gentlemen, that is only the impression I got from meeting the man. You, Dr. Seward, would likely be much better equipped to make estimations about him than would I.

"So the five of us attended several more of these clandestine gatherings, under the guidance of the Hooded Man. For several months, I looked forward to each new meeting. One night, I traveled to the appointed location as usual and found my four fellow students sitting there as I always did. This time, however, was different. The Hooded Man did not appear. We waited for nearly three hours before finally going our separate ways. That was the last we saw of our strange instructor. About one week later, I receieved a package, with no originating address, which contained *The Book of the Howling Eyes*, as you are now aware. You know the results of that book's arrival, just as I now know that Cromwell and Morse also received copies of the book. I think we can assume, having read of his scuffle with the police, that Cooper also had a copy of the book. I have neither read nor heard anything about Terence since that gathering."

"The powder contained in my copy of the book had a powerful effect upon me as well, but I seem to have a certain aptitude for the Hooded Man's methods, and so I was able to shrug off its effects once I had enjoyed the experiment for some time. I can certainly understand why the others, assuming they were less able to control their impulses before the powder became present, would give in so easily to its powers. It saddens me to hear of Abner Cromwell's death, but I must wonder why a man like him would engage in such activities to begin with. I do hope that Jacob Morse recovers fully from his ordeal. That, gentlemen, is all I know about this whole affair. I am afraid that I can be of no further help to you today."

Watson and Seward stood. Watson extended his hand to Bird.

"Mr. Bird, I'd like to thank you for your honesty and your willingness to share your story with us. You have been of great help to us. I would ask that you please keep us informed of the condition of your daughter. Please contact us if anything should occur involving either her or the others of whom we spoke today."

Bird shook Watson's hand and then Seward's. The two doctors left the Bird residence and made their way to Seward's hospital.

Chapter V:
The Jack Hendricks Experience

Watson and Seward sat in Seward's office. It was now late afternoon. They had arrived at the hospital an hour earlier and checked on the condition of Jacob Morse. There had been no change. They had stopped to eat some sandwiches that Sullivan had prepared and were now ready to resume discussion of their case and the story that had been related to them by Alexander Bird.

"Bird's story is believable enough, I suppose," Seward began. "We've both seen the effects of that powder for ourselves and it's not hard to believe, at least in my experience, that such a powder, teamed with a sufficiently dramatic presentation, could unhinge the minds of some individuals. I, at least, can assume that Mr. Bird was truthful in his telling of his tale. Do you concur, Watson?"

"I do," replied the older doctor. "Bird's story, and the evidence we've both seen so far, including the actions of Cromwell, Morse, and Clarice Bird, are all we have so far. I would agree that we should proceed on the assumption that all of this is true, at least until such a time that we are confronted with alternative information."

"So where do we go from here?" Seward asked.

Watson thought for a moment, and then began to reply.

"We must address this Whitechapel business, this murdered prostitute. Can it be coincidence that such an event would occur in the midst of all these other incidents, or are the two things connected?"

Seward nodded in agreement.

"We still have one member of the Hooded Man's little group who is unaccounted for; the man called Terence. Do you think he could be responsible for the murder? Is he our new version of Jack the Ripper?"

Watson lit his pipe and the scent of burning tobacco filled the little office.

"I think it's likely enough to be worth investigating," answered Watson. "I strongly suggest that we make our first order of business finding Terence!"

"But how do we go about it?" Seward, a bit puzzled, said. "We have only a first name, and while Terence is not as common a name as John, for example, there must be hundreds of them in London!"

"I have an idea," said Watson, "but we need more information. I need to know more about last night's murder...and I need some reference materials that I have in my room. Send your assistant Sullivan to fetch Inspector Lestrade and have them rendezvous with us at Baker Street."

Seward dispatched Sullivan on his task at once. The two doctors donned their hats and coats and left the hospital immediately. On the way to Baker Street, Watson cautioned Seward to choose his words carefully when in Lestrade's presence.

"Remember, Seward, that Lestrade does not know that the real Jack was caught and killed. Only the senior police who were involved in the case know that, as well as Holmes and I, and certain individuals connected to the government. Lestrade was not part of the original case. He knows only what is in the official record of those dreadful events."

An hour later, all four men were gathered at Baker Street; Watson and Seward had arrived first, followed by Sullivan and Lestrade. Seward thanked Sullivan for finding Lestrade so quickly and dismissed him to go back to the hospital and tend to the patients. Watson and Seward sat down and Lestrade followed their lead and did the same.

"So what was all the rush, gents?" the police inspector asked. "That fellow...what's his name again...Sullivan, said it was important. Have you found something out about all these crazies runnin' around lately?"

"Actually, Lestrade," Watson interrupted, "I wanted to ask you about the murder in Whitechapel last night."

Lestrade stood up; looking annoyed and began to turn towards the door as if to storm out.

"Enough with the damned Ripper business already; I had to dodge newspaper men all the way here! We don't know anything yet except that a woman got sliced up last night just off of Osborn Street, it was done like

"...the scent of burning tobacco filled the little office."

the Ripper used to do, and that's about it! It's only been half a day since the body was found and I've done nothin' but answer questions! How am I supposed to investigate the damned thing?"

Seward got up and put a hand on Lestrade's shoulder, applying just enough pressure to imply, in a friendly manner, that he should sit back down and relax.

"Inspector, please sit down. We don't wish to upset you. After all, we must all work together as you have worked with Dr. Watson and Mr. Holmes so many times in the past. I'm told, Inspector, that many of Holmes' most notable cases would never have been concluded without your very efficient involvement. Now we're asking you to come to our aid once more."

Seward's flattery worked and Lestrade returned to his chair, while Watson suppressed the urge to laugh.

"All right then, fellows, what can I do to be of help?" Lestrade asked, trying to sound humble, but not being very successful.

Watson stood up and began pacing as he spoke to Lestrade. Had he been able to observe himself, he might have realized that he was unintentionally imitating the mannerisms of Sherlock Holmes.

"Inspector Lestrade, I'm assuming that you have seen the original police files pertaining to the first series of killings credited to Jack the Ripper?"

Lestrade nodded. Watson continued.

"Tell me, Inspector, are the details of this latest slaying as similar as the newspapers and rumors are reporting to the first murders a decade ago?"

"Yes, Doctor," Lestrade confirmed. "The details are the same, right down to the things that were never told to the public the last time around. That's what makes it so ominous, Watson. It has to be the same maniac out there. He knows things…things that nobody else knows!"

Lestrade continued on for fifteen minutes, relating to Watson and Seward some of the most gruesome details of how the killing of Bess Fletcher had been accomplished. Luckily, Watson and Seward, after years in the medical profession, both had developed strong stomachs and great tolerance for terrible detail. When Lestrade had finished his explanation of the murder, Watson and Seward thanked him profusely and he left their company.

When the inspector had left the building, Watson took his seat again and the two resumed their planning of the next steps in the investigation.

"That settles it, Seward. We've narrowed the field of potential Terences!" said Watson with some satisfaction.

Seward did not quite follow Watson's logic.

"How does Lestrade's report help?"

Watson laughed a bit.

"Seward, you sound like me! Holmes often tells me things that cause me to pause and ask for an explanation. We know, though Lestrade does not, that Jack the Ripper is dead. Obviously, he cannot be the killer of Bess Fletcher. We also now know that the details of the crime were such that it could not be a member of the general public who committed the murder. It was an exact or nearly exact duplication of the Ripper's methods, not a mere imitation based upon newspaper reports. This means that our suspect must have a more than general knowledge of the original killings; he had to have been involved in the investigation of the initial slaying spree!"

Seward nodded. He now understood.

"So you believe the killer is a policeman!" Seward said. "But how do we find out which one? As we said earlier, Terence is not an uncommon name; surely there must be more than one at Scotland Yard."

"I'll return in a few moments," said Watson, and he vanished behind the door of one of the apartment's other rooms.

From the main room, Seward could hear sounds of activity from behind that closed door; things being moved around, boxes being opened and closed, papers being shuffled and tossed aside. A few minutes later, Watson emerged carrying a large bundle of papers. Seward could see that the words upon the papers were handwritten. Watson sat down and looked through the stack until he found the right section of his notes.

"What is that?" Seward asked him.

Watson held up the sheet he had selected as he explained.

"As you know, I've made it a serious hobby to keep a careful record of my experiences of involvement in the cases of Sherlock Holmes. Many of those records have been published for the enjoyment of the public... and to help better Holmes' reputation, which has resulted in more cases coming to us. I do keep a record of every case, Seward, even those that can never, for one reason or another, be revealed to anyone else. These are the notes from the first Jack the Ripper case, although I did find it proper, considering the oath I took before the queen, to destroy some of these notes. Give me a moment please, and I shall, hopefully, have found a piece of information that will accelerate the progress of our investigation tremendously."

Seward sat and waited as Watson sifted through the pages of his bundle of decade-old notes. The minutes ticked by on the apartment's clock.

"Eureka!" shouted Watson, using an old Greek phrase which meant 'I've found it!' "The man we must find is a Chief Inspector Terence Hendricks. He was the only member of the team of investigators who bore that name. Assuming Bird's fellow student of demonology was not using an alias, and assuming that our theory about a connection between the mysterious powder and the apparent resurrection of Jack the Ripper is correct, this must be the man we seek!"

Watson stood and went to the window. He opened it and stuck his head out, looking out along Baker Street. Spotting one of the people who could suit his purposes, he shouted out to the street below.

"Charlie! Charlie, up here! Be a good boy and hurry up here, lad! There's money in my hand if you'll do a little job for us!"

Seconds later, swift, enthusiastic footsteps were heard coming up the stairs. The door to the room flew open and a dirty-faced boy of about eleven trotted in. His clothes were cheap and tattered and his shoes were worn and muddy.

"Yes, Sir, Dr. Watson," the child said. "What do you need?"

Young Charlie was a member of the Baker Street Irregulars, a group of street urchins who often did favors for Holmes and Watson, since boys could run quickly through the crowded streets or sneak about in places that would be more difficult for a grown man to go unnoticed.

Watson handed a few small coins to the boy.

"Wait one moment, Charlie. I'll have a note for you to deliver as soon as it's written."

He grabbed a sheet of paper from the desk and scrawled a brief note.

"Lestrade, I need information. What is the present status and address of a Chief Inspector Terence Hendricks? Come to 221 B at once when you know the answers. It is most urgent! Watson."

The note was soon folded and placed in the waiting hand of Charlie.

"Go and find Inspector Lestrade and give this to him, Lad," said Watson.

Charlie made a face.

"Lestrade; what do ya' want that crummy old copper for? He's always chasin' after us and accusin' us of bein' loiterers! I don't know what that means, but it's downright insultin' and I don't like it one bit!"

Watson laughed.

"Just deliver the note, Charlie, or I'll find another boy who wants that money!"

Charlie darted out the door, note in hand and coins in the other. Watson knew the lad would get the job done. Those energetic urchins always did.

Watson and Seward waited for what felt like hours. It was growing late in the day and they worried that time was running out. If Hendricks really was the new Ripper, they had to find him as soon as possible, before he decided to stalk the foggy London night again, to seek out and slay another woman. Mrs. Hudson brought them some tea and they smoked and talked while they waited, hoping that Lestrade would soon be coming up the stairs of 221 Baker Street.

The teapot was empty and the remnants of tea in each of the doctor's cups were growing cold when they finally heard the pounding of footsteps on the stairs. Watson could tell by the sound of the steps that it was an adult ascending to their floor and not young Charlie returning to report failure. Watson could only hope that it was the expected detective and not some potential new client looking for Sherlock Holmes.

Watson's hopes were rewarded as Lestrade, looking tired and ruffled, walked in and made his way to the one remaining unoccupied chair, plopping himself down without so much as a polite greeting.

"You look terrible, Inspector," Seward observed. "It must have been a busy day for your entire department."

"Panic in the streets, Doctor," said the exhausted inspector, "Panic in the streets. If we don't figure this new Ripper business out soon, the people are likely to break down the doors of Scotland Yard and lynch us all for not keeping the streets safe!"

Watson interrupted Lestrade's complaining.

"I'm sorry for your tiredness, Inspector, but I need to know, what did you learn of Terence Hendricks?"

Lestrade took his small notebook from his pocket and flipped it open.

"Chief Inspector Hendricks retired from the force five years ago. He is now sixty-two years of age. I have his last known address here. What is the significance of this man anyway, Watson?"

Watson stood up and walked over to the window. He parted the curtains to look outside and answered Lestrade's inquiry as he did so.

"Assuming a certain wild theory of mine and Seward's is correct, Lestrade, this retired police inspector may very well be the man who murdered that woman in Whitechapel last night."

Lestrade jumped up from his chair, forgetting his tiredness and suddenly rejuvenated.

"Well then what're we waiting for, doctors? Let's go and arrest the bloody bastard! They'll give me his old rank for sure if I bring him in. I'll be Chief Inspector Lestrade if I'm the man to catch Jack the Ripper!"

Watson stopped him before his glee went beyond the boundaries of civilized conversation.

"Wait a minute, Lestrade. I didn't say that Hendricks was Jack the Ripper, just that he might have killed that one woman. Now we haven't any proof of any wrongdoing yet, so we can't just barge into the man's home and arrest him! What we have to do is go and watch his residence. It's getting dark now, so we should be going. Will you be joining us, Inspector?"

Lestrade was already putting on his hat.

"I wouldn't miss this chance for anything, Watson! Even if he only killed that one girl, I'll be a hero if I bring him in. Hurry up, boys!"

Lestrade bolted out the door like a hound after a fox, with Watson and Seward grabbing their coats and following after him. They both instinctively felt inside their coats to be sure they had their revolvers with them.

The three investigators made their way to the neighborhood in which the retired inspector resided. They located the appropriate house and found positions in which to wait and watch. Having determined that the house had both a front and rear door, they divided their forces. Seward snuck to the area behind the house and hid between some fairly tall bushes in order to watch the back door. Watson found a bench across the street and several houses down where he could sit and maintain a clear view of the front of Hendricks' house. Anyone who saw him there would simply think he was a middle-aged gentleman taking a rest during a walk. Lestrade, the real policeman among the three, and therefore the one who could most easily dispel any suspicion of odd behavior, would wander around the area, discreetly keeping an eye on the locations of both Watson and Seward, so that if Hendricks left the house and one doctor followed him, Lestrade could alert the other, so that all three could then join in the pursuit.

The dark of night had fallen completely on London as the three took up their positions. Lestrade's information had suggested that Hendricks lived alone, as he was a widower, so when Seward saw the glow of a lamp inside the house, he thought it safe to assume that Hendricks was indeed at home.

Inside the fairly large home, Terence Hendricks sat in his home office, which was lit by the single lamp he had just ignited. The room was lined with bookshelves and souvenirs of his long, illustrious career as a police officer, but he no longer cared about those trinkets of past glories. As far as he was concerned, the old chief inspector was dead and buried. He was a new man, a different person, reborn and reshaped by the miracle brought on by the Navigators of the Inner Planes and the wondrous power of *The Book of the Howling Eyes.*

The experience he had lived through thanks to the potency of the secrets held within that magical tome had transformed him, phoenix-like, into what he was now, a spirit of vengeance and power, brought to London to cleanse the streets of their obscene filth, of the women whose selfish actions left a great stain on the city's streets, night after night. He had to destroy them all. He was, after all, a pure instrument of God's wrath. This he knew because the voices told him so, and he had to follow their divine commands!

He had taken his ceremonial bath, cleansing his body and his mind in preparation of what was to be done soon. He had dressed in his finest clothes, attire befitting an angel given human form. Now he sat and he shined his tools, the blades of death and justice. Soon he would conceal them in his cloak, to be brought forth at the moment when his task was at hand.

As the time passed and the night wore on, the flow of traffic and pedestrians lessened and Watson and Lestrade began to worry that the absence of more people in the area would make them begin to look conspicuous. Their worries soon fell by the wayside as the front door of the house opened and a lone figure emerged. He was fairly tall, strongly built, walking out the door in a slow, steady, confident manner. He wore a long black coat and a top hat. He reached the end of his walkway and turned left, heading down the street. Watson spotted him first and removed his hat, a signal that had been worked out in advance. Lestrade saw the signal and then saw Hendricks in movement. He made certain that Hendricks could not see him and then darted past the house to the area behind it. He found Seward there, still watching the rear of the building.

"Seward, he's left the house!" said Lestrade excitedly. "Watson and I shall follow him while you look around in his house. Find a way in; break a window if you must. I'll see that no blame comes your way."

With that, Seward began to look for a means of admittance to the house. Lestrade went back out front to join Watson in the pursuit of Terence Hendricks.

Seward did as Lestrade had suggested and immediately began to try to get inside. He went to the back door, but was not surprised to find it locked. Not wishing to waste time, he took off his coat, wrapped it around his forearm so as not to injure himself, and smashed the door's window. Taking care to avoid the jagged edges of the shattered glass, he reached inside and unlocked the door. It swung open and he crept inside. He found himself in the kitchen and began to look for a way to gain some light with which to inspect the home's interior. He found an oil lamp on the table and lit it with a match he had carried with him in his pocket. Light, a small amount but enough to give him a clear view of his surroundings, began to glow in the room. He glanced around, seeing just an ordinary kitchen. He left that room and found the hallway that led to the rest of the house.

The parlor seemed typical of a house of that size in that particular area of the city, as did the bedroom. The entire home was sparsely decorated, obviously the living quarters of an unmarried man or, in this case, a widower.

Finally, Seward found the retired inspector's office. He immediately knew that this was where Hendricks usually spent most of his time. The place had the look of a room filled with the things that a man liked to keep close at hand; his books, his mementos of old times, writing materials, and other such things. Seward placed the lamp atop Hendricks' desk and sat down in the chair behind it. He began to look through the desk's single drawer. He found what he had expected to find; *The Book of the Howling Eyes*. Just as all the others had, the copy in the desk had the torn endpaper indicative of the release of the mind-altering powder that Watson and Seward had, themselves, been temporarily victimized by.

There was nothing else worth noting inside the desk drawer. Seward put the book back and closed the drawer. He began to get up from the chair, but as he did so he felt his foot brush against something under the desk. He reached down and found a small wooden case. He placed it on the desk and opened the box. It was a surgeon's kit; a portable set of surgical instruments of the type that Watson had most probably used when in the military. It contained scalpels and knives of various shapes and sizes. If Hendricks was not the new Ripper, Seward thought to himself, what was he doing with a set of surgical blades? To further convince Seward that his and Watson's theory had more than a little validity, the largest of the kit's knives was missing. Presumably, Seward suspected, Hendricks had taken the knife with him when he had left the house. Even more than before, Seward hoped that Watson and Lestrade would use caution should they find it necessary to confront the man!

Several blocks away now, Hendricks continued his slow, steady walking pace along the streets of London. Watson and Lestrade followed behind him, far enough to avoid arousing suspicion in Hendricks, but close enough to hopefully avoid losing sight of him in the shadows of the darkened streets. Hendricks and his unnoticed followers travelled on through the streets of the retired policeman's home neighborhood, through the surrounding blocks, and slowly moved into an area of the city that was less polished, less well-reputed, and more of a hive of those whom proper society considered to be less than desirable company. As they moved from one area to the next, the number of people that were around them, walking around on the nighttime streets, actually increased. This was the part of London where the night was the day and the people of the shadows came out to deal in businesses that were looked down upon by the law and those citizens who preferred to conduct themselves honestly.

It occurred to Watson, as they walked, that perhaps they should have disguised themselves to fit in better in such a place. Surely, he thought, that is what Sherlock Holmes would have done, but it was too late for that now. On they walked, never taking their eyes off Terence Hendricks, except to occasionally glance around in case some stealthy pickpocket should try to add the contents of their pockets to the contents of his.

They passed two women standing there, leaning on the side of a building. Watson correctly guessed them to be prostitutes. As he and Lestrade passed, one of them stepped forward, smiling a grin that showed an unsightly gap where one of her front teeth should have been.

"Lonely this fine evening, gentlemen?" she asked as the held out her hand towards them.

"Outta the way or I'll have you locked up!" said Lestrade rather brusquely and he and Watson kept going. As they walked, they could hear her yelling loudly at them in the background.

"Aye, you won't need we then, will ya? A pair o' buggers you must be!"

The encounter with the two "ladies" over, they looked up ahead and tightened their focus on Hendricks. There were more prostitutes around now; two over there, one here, a few more on the other side of the street. It was quite an adequate selection for anyone who was interested in what they were selling. Many of them seemed to be looking at Lestrade and Watson, as those two men were the best dressed in the area. Up ahead, Hendricks was receiving similar attention. Watson and Lestrade saw Hendricks stop and begin to talk to one of the women, a tall and dreadfully thin young girl. They paused for a second, not wanting to go too close to their target until they were certain that he was something other than a normal client of those women. Not wishing to appear to have stopped for nothing, Watson took out his pipe and feigned an act of fumbling while trying to light it. As he acted, Lestrade kept watch on Hendricks.

Moments later, it appeared from Lestrade's vantage point that a deal had been struck between the woman and her new customer. The pair disappeared between two buildings. Watson and Lestrade headed in that direction. They reached the point where Hendricks and the girl had changed course and followed. The alley was dark and ended at a solid wall. The doctor and the inspector turned right, which was the only way available. They walked quickly along the rear wall of the building which they were now behind. As they emerged from the darkness of the alleys, they saw the pair they sought. The girl was against the wall facing Hendricks. He was reaching into his coat as if to take out the money for their transaction, but he instead produced his large surgical knife.

The prostitute screamed.

"Halt!" shouted Inspector Lestrade. Watson drew his revolver, as did Lestrade.

Hendricks whirled. His eyes were wild and his mouth was opened wide. His hat flew off and he turned, revealing a head of thick, bushy gray hair. He held his blade out in front of him. The girl screamed again when she saw the two newcomers and their guns.

"Step away from the girl!" Lestrade commanded Hendricks.

Hendricks just glared at him.

"I know you, don't I?" said the retired policeman, now the new Jack the Ripper. "Yes, yes I do! I can't recall your name, but you're a policeman! You were younger when I knew you. You haven't aged much; perhaps you're not as human as you might appear to be to others! Yes, yes, that's the answer isn't it? You're a guardian sent by the devil to stop me, to keep me from my task, to save the life of this wretched specimen of femaleness! I fear you not!"

Hendricks turned away from Lestrade and Watson and back to the girl. He raised his knife. A shot rang out! The Ripper fell forward as Lestrade's bullet tore violently into his back. The prostitute screamed again.

Lestrade and Watson ran towards the place where Hendricks had fallen.

"Run away from here and thank God your blood isn't staining his knife, young lady!" said Watson to the girl, and she listened, fleeing the scene.

Lestrade kicked the dropped surgical knife clear of Hendricks' reach. It slid harmlessly until the wall stopped its journey along the ground.

Watson knelt down to examine Hendricks. Blood was seeping through the back of the old inspector's coat. Lestrade helped Watson turn the injured man, who was quite heavy, over. Watson cradled Hendricks' head as the murderer gasped with his last breath.

"I come back to thee now, Oh Lord!"

Terence Hendricks was dead. There would be no more Ripper-like murders on the streets of London now. Lestrade wondered how he would explain these events in his report.

"Watson, leave the scene. Go find Seward and get on with your investigation. I'm not telling you this out of any desire to claim all the credit as my own, but the fewer people involved in this mess, the easier it will be to make it all be forgotten as quickly as possible."

Watson nodded, stood up, and walked back out of the alleyway. As he returned to the street, he heard Lestrade blow his whistle, a signal that any other police in the area should make their way to where he was.

After searching Hendricks' house, Seward had gone back outside and concealed himself in the bushes again. Not knowing when Watson or Lestrade might return, and not knowing precisely where they had gone, he could think of no better idea than to wait there. He estimated that nearly an hour had now passed and he was growing worried.

Finally, he heard the familiar voice of Watson calling out to him.

"Seward, Seward, are you still here, friend?"

Assuming, based upon the volume of Watson's call, that there was no longer any need for sneaking about, Seward emerged from his hiding place and walked towards the sound of Watson's voice. The two met on the street.

"What happened?" Seward asked.

Watson began to explain.

"Hendricks is dead. Our theory was correct. He talked a prostitute into going behind a building with him and he tried to cut her to pieces. Lestrade and I interrupted him. He accused Lestrade of being a devil sent to keep him from accomplishing his work, whatever that may have been in his distorted vision of reality. He went back to trying to attack the woman… and Lestrade shot him. He was dead in moments."

"And you're both unhurt?" asked Seward with some concern, as he had noted Lestrade's absence.

"We're fine," Watson answered. "Lestrade summoned his fellow policemen and he's taking care of the official parts of this ugly business now. He vowed to keep any mention of the two of us out of it. He'll probably be hailed as a hero, which is fine as far as I'm concerned. He's a good man. Though he lacks the intellect of a Sherlock Holmes, his intentions are good and he's often a credit to Scotland Yard. What did you find in Hendricks' house?"

"The things we expected to find," Seward replied. "That infernal book was there of course, as well as most of a surgeon's kit."

"Yes," said Watson, "the rest of that set was in the hand of Hendricks when he was shot. It's gotten late, Seward. We'll part ways now and meet again tomorrow. I'll come by the hospital in the morning. We must decide on our next step."

Chapter VI:
A Bird in the Hand

As Watson and Seward were each making their way to their respective homes for the night, Alexander Bird sat in his study and stared straight ahead, expressionless, as if he were staring into infinity. He had not slept in days. When he had assured his two visitors that he exercised perfect control over the effects of the strange, mind-altering powder, he had lied. He may have managed to maintain possession of his senses during the waking hours of the day, but in sleep, or attempts to sleep, Alexander Bird was a haunted man. The moment he drifted into slumber, the dreams would begin. There was nothing he could do to stop them.

He had finally given up on his attempts to get through a night of sleep. Instead, he sat in his office looking straight ahead, but not really seeing anything at all. The powder's effect on his mind had dredged up things he had not wanted to be confronted with; dark thoughts, desires, fantasies and dreams that he desperately wanted to suppress and send back to the depths of memory and thought from which they had come. Try as he might, he could not stop thinking of the images and ideas that the powder had brought back to his conscious mind. As he sat behind his desk, his mind began to twist and bend again, swirling into the darkness of his deepest hidden self.

In the background, he could hear the piano keys striking, pounding out that weird, unearthly music that was the result of his daughter's accidental exposure to the powder. Bird cursed at himself for having brought that infernal substance into his home and to his family. Not only was he faced with his own darkness, but he had infected his own child with its strange influence as well. His heart and mind filled with overwhelming guilt and shame.

He stood up and walked to the center of the room. He moved a chair into a spot just below the middle of a long, thick wooden beam that ran across the room's ceiling. He stood on the chair and tugged on the beam to judge its ability to hold weight. He nodded when he had estimated its threshold. He got down off the chair and walked over to the window, detaching from the window the rope that he had used to pull the curtains open when he wished to admit sunlight to the room. He tossed the rope up, over the beam, and manufactured a loop from one end of it. He got back up upon the chair, breathed in deeply, and did what his despair was urging him to do. Moments later, Alexander Bird was dead.

Watson was deep in his slumber, having arrived back at Baker Street in a state of utter exhaustion after the confrontation with, and resulting death of, Terence Hendricks. He had gone immediately to bed and drifted off to sleep wondering if, by some miracle, he might manage to sleep later than usual into the morning hours. He was destined to be disappointed.

"Dr. Watson, are you awake? Dr. Watson?"

The voice of Mrs. Hudson, at quite a loud volume for so early in the morning, shattered Watson's unconscious peace and he sat upright in bed, muttering a minor profanity. He stood, pulled on his robe and walked out into the main room, opening the door.

"Yes, Mrs. Hudson, I'm awake," he said with sarcasm. "What is so important at this early hour?"

The landlady shoved an envelope into Watson's hand.

"A messenger just left this for you, Sir. He said it was very, very urgent, so I thought it best to give it to you right away. I'll go brew you some tea."

Watson nodded as he began to open the letter.

"You did the right thing Mrs. Hudson. Thank you. And perhaps you should make that coffee instead of tea today."

He turned and went over to his chair to read the single sheet of paper that had been inside the envelope.

"Dr. Watson,

Based upon your several visits to our home, I assume you have some understanding of the strange events which have been recently occurring in our household. Something has happened. I beg you and your friend, Dr. Seward, to come at once.

Mrs. Dorothea Bird"

Watson tossed the note down on the desk, dressed, and was out the door as quickly as possible. He hired a cab, collected Seward, who was already up, at the hospital, and the two men proceeded to the Bird residence.

Mrs. Bird opened the door moments after Watson had knocked. She greeted Watson and Seward and they both could immediately tell that she had been crying.

"Come in, please, doctors," she implored them.

They followed her in and she sat down, motioning for them both to do the same. When they all were seated, she looked at them and spoke.

"Alexander committed suicide last night, by hanging. I discovered his body when I woke this morning."

Watson was stunned.

"Oh my," he said. "Mrs. Bird, you have our most sincere condolences."

Seward, not wishing to simply repeat what Watson had already said, asked the obvious question.

"Did he leave a note of any sort, any indication of why he would want to do such a dreadful thing?"

Mrs. Bird simply shook her head and tears began to stream from her eyes again. Watson stood and took his handkerchief from his pocket, offering it to the weeping widow.

"Where is your daughter, Clarice, Mrs. Bird? How has she reacted to this terrible event?"

Mrs. Bird's weeping intensified.

"As soon as I told her of her father's fate, she went into her room and has not yet emerged. I fear for her state of mind, Doctor, but I hesitate to try to coax her out of her solitude. She's been acting so strangely ever since the piano playing began. That was part of the reason I was inclined to summon the two of you. You seemed to have had some understanding of what has happened to her of late. I thought perhaps you could help us."

Watson nodded his agreement.

"Of course, Mrs. Bird; Dr. Seward and I would be happy to do anything we can. John, shall we go to the young Miss Bird and see how she is?"

Seward stood and he and Watson ascended the staircase to the second floor of the house. They passed the open door of a large bedroom and assumed it belonged to Mr. and Mrs. Bird. They stopped in front of the next door, which was closed, and Seward knocked gently.

"Yes, Mother?" came a voice from behind the door.

"Miss Bird…Clarice…this is not your mother. It's John Seward, one of the doctors who came to see you play the piano. Do you remember me,

Miss Bird? My friend, Dr. Watson and I are here. May we come in?"

Through the door, they could hear the sound of footsteps coming towards them. The knob twisted and the door opened. Clarice Bird was standing there, fully dressed and with a semi-smile on her face, not looking at all like the inconsolable, weeping girl they had expected to see.

"Hello, doctors," she said warmly and stepped out into the hallway to join them.

"Miss Bird," said Seward, "we wish to offer our most sincere sympathy on this terrible and sudden loss. If there is anything that either I or Dr. Watson can do to make this dreadful time easier for you and your mother, all you must do is ask."

Clarice nodded and smiled.

"I wish to be honest with you both, as you have been very kind to me, most unlike the others who came here to stare at me or try to profit from my musical abilities. While my father's death is indeed sudden and tragic, I must confess to feeling less grief and more relief since my mother's terrible discovery today."

"Relief?" asked Watson with shock. "Why would you be relieved? Is there something that we have not been told? Was your father ill?"

"No, Dr. Watson," she answered. "I am greatly saddened by my father's death, and especially by the way in which it occurred…but that grief and loss is overshadowed by the fact that, for the first time in many days, I feel like myself again. I am not quite sure how to express my feelings in words, but it is as though the shock of what had happened had shattered the strange, dreamlike trance that has held me captive since that night when I began to play the piano so suddenly. I can think clearly again…and for that I am grateful, though I will miss my father terribly. I am, perhaps, somewhat ashamed to feel so happy!"

Seward reached out and took hold of her hand in a reassuring manner.

"Miss Bird, you have no need to be ashamed of anything. It has been my experience that abrupt shock may sometimes have such an effect on the mind, just as a man who has been timid and even cowardly might suddenly rise to great heights of heroism when confronted by the horrors of war. If you are indeed feeling better and are able to think clearly once again, then we are glad of that fact, though tragic are the events that led to this new clarity."

"Miss Bird," Watson added to the conversation, "I hope you will forgive my curiosity, but have you tried to play the piano since hearing of your father's death? I apologize if that sounds callous."

Clarice shook her head.

"No, Doctor, I haven't, but I can see why you would ask such a question. Will you join me in the parlor? I should like to try."

The doctors followed her down the stairs. As they began their walk, Watson noticed that Seward and Miss Bird both hesitated for a moment before letting go of each other's hand. Had the two of them suddenly felt an attraction to each other, he wondered? Seward was ten or twelve years older than Clarice, Watson estimated, but he had seen people with greater differences in age come together before. For a moment, their actions reminded him of his meeting his late wife, Mary Morstan, for the first time, during a case he had participated in during his earlier days with Sherlock Holmes, a case he had called *The Sign of Four*. For a brief moment, Watson was lost in memory, but he quickly came back to alertness as the trio entered the Bird family's parlor.

Clarice sat down at the piano. Watson and Seward stood and watched. Clarice's fingers hovered over the keys, but she hesitated to make contact. From behind her, Seward could see that she was trembling a bit. Finally, one fingertip came down and touched a white key. Then a second key was pressed. Her speed increased and a flurry of notes emerged into the room's air…but there was nothing musical about it! It sounded like an off-key string of plinking sounds and made Watson wince.

Clarice stopped. She held her hands in front of her and simply stared down at the piano. Thinking her upset, Seward stepped forward and was about to put a hand on her shoulder to console her, but she surprised him by jumping up from the piano bench and whirling around towards him, grinning.

"It's gone, it's gone!" she said, overjoyed. "I don't know which keys to press anymore; the curse has been lifted! It was terrible! I felt like a slave, a slave to that frightful music…but I don't know how to make that music anymore!"

She grabbed hold of Seward and hugged him. He tried, for a second, to push her away, suddenly aware that what was happening might look improper, but then he realized that her joyful outburst had suddenly turned into sobs; she was crying.

"My God," she whimpered. "My father, my father is dead."

Watson just watched. He was glad to see that the tragic death of Alexander Bird had had at least one positive effect; it had returned his daughter to normalcy. Perhaps, he said to himself, she will not be a permanent victim of that terrible powder, as Abner Cromwell was.

"It's gone, it's gone!" she said, overjoyed.

Once the piano experiment had proven that Clarice Bird was seemingly free of the effects of the mind-altering powder, Watson and Seward rejoined Mrs. Bird, who had made them some tea. The suddenly widowed woman seemed to have composed herself somewhat. Tears no longer ran down her cheeks and she was no longer shaking with shock. They made polite conversation for a short time, until Watson decided that it was time to get back to the business of investigating recent events.

"Mrs. Bird," he said, "I apologize if this request seems rude, but would you be willing to allow us to examine the contents of your husband's office? It may help bring to light the reasons why this tragedy has occurred."

"That would be quite all right, Doctor," she answered.

Watson and Seward went into Alexander Bird's study and closed the door behind them. They both noticed that the foul stench of death still hung in the air. Watson examined the volumes on the bookshelves while Seward sat down behind Bird's desk and opened the drawer.

Seward took out Bird's copy of *The Book of the Howling Eyes* and placed it upon the desk.

"Here it is," he said with disgust in his voice, "that damnable book, the cause of all this grief. Unfortunately for our investigation, there seems to be nothing else of much interest in this desk."

"It's the same story with these books," Watson added. "There's nothing here but business ledgers and common literary works. I was hoping to find something that could hint at the location of the meeting place of this group that Bird and the others belonged to, but there seems to be no such clue here."

Seward put the book inside his jacket.

"I'm not going to leave this book here. I see no reason to let it sit here and upset either Mrs. Bird or Clarice should they happen upon it while going through the deceased's possessions. I shall take it back to the hospital with me and burn it!"

They left the Bird residence and took a cab back to Seward's hospital. Watson noted the way Seward smiled as he bid farewell to the young Miss Bird, but he said nothing of the matter to the younger doctor.

As they rode through the London Streets, conversation turned to the direction in which their inquiries would have to turn next.

"We have now encountered all of the members of that little group except for one. Hendricks, Cromwell and Bird are dead. Jacob Morse still insists that he is that Baalzephon character and shows no sign of improvement," Seward recounted where things stood.

"We would be wise," Watson suggested, "in trying to find out what has become of Edwin Cooper, the banker. He was arrested by the police after his violent outburst in the streets, but because he was not deemed as insane as Cromwell or Morse, he was never brought to a facility such as yours. We must learn what has become of him and attempt to arrange a meeting."

Seward nodded in agreement.

They arrived at the hospital a short time later. It was still fairly early in the day and neither of them had eaten yet. The hospital's cook made two omelets. After breakfast, plans were made for the furthering of the investigation. Seward would remain at the hospital and try, yet again, to wade through the muck of Jacob Morse's state of mind and find some useful information. Watson, meanwhile, would seek out Inspector Lestrade and find out what had become of Edwin Cooper since his outburst and arrest. Watson was on his way immediately after the morning meal was concluded.

In another part of London, the tall, thin man walked down the long corridor where he frequently went to make reports to his superior. He knocked three times on the usual door and it creaked open just enough for sound to easily pass from corridor to room, but not wide enough for the thin man to see inside. He still had never seen the face of the one to whom he reported, only a hand, a wrinkled, aged, long-fingered hand.

"What has happened?" asked the voice from behind the door.

"An interesting occurrence," said the thin man. "Alexander Bird has killed himself, though that was expected. His daughter, however, has undergone a change. The shock of her father's death seems to have counteracted the effect of the dust! She has lost her ability to play the piano and her mind seems to have cleared. She was given no drugs or other cures, yet she has returned to normalcy."

"Most unfortunate," said the voice. "That is an unexpected development. I had thought I understood the course that the effects of exposure to the powder would run. I should like to examine the girl in person. Bring her to me!"

The thin man did not reply. He did not have to. His masters knew that he would not refuse a task. The thin man turned and went back the way he had come, already beginning to plan a way to carry out his new assignment.

Dr. Seward and his chief orderly, Sullivan, stood outside the cell where Jacob Morse was being held. There had been no noticeable change in Morse's condition. When Seward and Sullivan had first arrived to check on his progress, he had been sitting there, staring straight ahead with a look of intensity on his face. When he noticed the presence of his two watchers, he stood, walked to the little glassless window on the door and shouted at them.

"Release me! I command you again! Baalzephon must go free!"

Sullivan laughed out loud.

"This one doesn't give up easy, does 'e, Doctor?"

Seward did not reply to Sullivan's comment. He was lost in thought, scratching his chin while considering what to do next.

"Sullivan," said Seward, "I'm tired of watching him pace and listening to him scream at us. Let's restrain him fully. We'll sedate him too and maybe then we can get him to make some sense. You go in fast and hold him down. I'll drug him. Be careful though; remember how he tried to bite Watson!"

Sullivan stuck his key into the door's lock and turned it. He shoved the door open and rushed inside, grabbing hold of Morse and pushing him down onto the bed. Seward was right behind him and pulled a small vial of liquid from his pocket. As Morse began to scream and struggle, Sullivan used all his strength to hold him down. Though Morse was slim and did not look very strong, his lunacy added to his strength and made his restraint a formidable task even for the stocky Irish orderly. Seward leaned over the struggling men and unceremoniously dumped the contents of the vial into Morse's open mouth. Some of the liquid sedative dribbled down his chin and onto his shirt, but he swallowed enough of it to, within minutes, fall into a noticeably weakened state and slump into near-unconsciousness. Sullivan strapped him down, at the wrists, ankles and neck, to the bed.

"We'll wait an hour and come back and see if he's returned to partial wakefulness. He should be easier to communicate with if that is the case. Go have a smoke, Sullivan. You've earned it," Seward said, and turned and left the cell.

An hour later, he re-entered Morse's cell. Sullivan stood outside in case he should be needed. Seward sat down on the edge of the bed and looked down at his dazed patient. Morse had opened his eyes, but appeared to be in a dreamlike, half-awake state.

"Can you hear me?" Seward asked him.

There was no reply for several minutes, as if Morse were trying to decide if he really was awake, at least partially, or if Seward was some apparition that might appear during the slumbers of late evening or early morning.

"I...can..." answered the young man's slurred voice.

"What is your name?" was Seward's next question.

Morse's eyes flickered back and forth several times.

"Jacob. Jacob Morse."

"Good, son, very good," Seward said reassuringly. "What is your occupation?"

Morse let out a low moaning sound before answering. In Seward's estimation, he was slowly returning to some sort of state of lucidity.

"I sell canvasses and oils and brushes to artists."

Seward nodded.

"Jacob, do you recognize the name Baalzephon? Can you tell me who that is?"

Morse's eyes widened. He looked as if fear had suddenly rushed into his thoughts.

"I am Baalzephon. No, no, I am not! He was me...but I was not he! I...I don't know, I don't know? He is gone...but where? In or out...I don't know!"

Seward stood up and paced about the room for a few minutes. He carefully considered his next words as he allowed Morse a bit of time to calm down. Finally, he returned to his seat at the edge of the bed.

"Jacob, I want you to listen carefully to me. This is the first time I have spoken to you when you have been aware of your true name. Please allow me to introduce myself. My name is John Seward and I am a doctor. I want to help you. Let me assure you that you truly are Jacob Morse, you are a seller of artist's supplies, and you are twenty-six years old. For some time now, you have been ill, suffering from delusions that you are someone other than who I know you to be. Your condition seems to be improving somewhat today, and I wish to help you further this recovery in any way that I can. Do you understand me, Jacob?"

The patient nodded the best he could, hampered as he was by the restraints that Sullivan had applied.

Several miles away from Seward's hospital, Dr. Watson was led by Inspector Lestrade down the corridor of holding cells in the basement of one of London's many police precinct houses. He glanced into many of the cells as they passed and saw that most of those temporarily imprisoned there were the typical miscreants that one would expect to see there; pickpockets, drunkards, a few prostitutes, and other minor offenders of the law. They stopped in front of the very last cell and Lestrade motioned in the direction of the small, barred chamber.

"Dr. Watson, I present to you Mr. Edwin Cooper."

Watson looked in. He saw a man of about thirty-five years. He was tall and strongly built. His chin showed that he had not had a shave for at least several days. Despite his look of physical toughness, the man's face looked gentle and kind, though tired and immensely sad.

"Are you a lawyer, Sir?" asked Edwin Cooper with desperation in his voice and longing in his eyes.

"No, Mr. Cooper, my name is John Watson and I am a physician. May I come in and speak with you?"

Lestrade unlocked and opened the cell door without waiting for Cooper's reply. Watson stepped inside and Lestrade closed the door behind him. The inspector stood outside, keeping an attentive eye on the cell's two occupants.

Watson sat down and began to speak to Cooper.

"I'm not going to waste time with pleasantries, Cooper. I need information…and you are clearly in need of some help yourself. Let me assure you from the start that there is no need to hide anything from me. I know all about your little group of students of the occult and your secret meetings with the Hooded Man. I know about *The Book of the Howling Eyes* and the strange powder concealed therein. I know, from a bit of my own experience, of the dangerous effects of that dusty substance and I know that that is what caused the violent outburst that led you to be locked up in this tiny cell. I want to help you if I can, Cooper, but I ask that you help me in return."

"What can I do?" Cooper asked without hesitation.

"To begin," said Watson, "you can answer some questions. I am assuming that you were exposed to the powder, which was what caused your unfortunate outburst and encounter with the police. Why, Mr. Cooper, do you seem as if the effect has gone? I'm afraid your fellow students were not so fortunate."

"I believe, Doctor," Cooper responded, "that I must have inhaled only a small amount of the stuff, which I'm glad was the case. I had the good fortune to have opened the book outdoors as well as the sense to try to avoid the stuff once it erupted from the book. Dr. Watson, when you said that the others had not been so fortunate, what did you mean? What has become of them?"

Watson sighed.

"Young Jacob Morse is being kept in a mental asylum, suffering from delusions of being some sort of hell-born demon. The others are dead. Alexander Bird hanged himself just last night. Abner Cromwell terribly mutilated himself and later committed suicide. The man you knew as Terence savagely murdered a woman and was shot dead by the police when he tried to duplicate the crime with another victim."

"My God!" said Cooper excitedly, and then bowed his head in sadness. That's terrible, terrible. What more do you want to know, Doctor? I shall help you in any way that I can."

Watson was relieved at Cooper's state of mind, which seemed clear, at least in his estimation, and at Cooper's willingness to help.

"To begin with," said Watson, "can you tell me how to find the Hooded Man?"

Cooper shook his head.

"I don't know how to contact him. I just know where we met him for those meetings."

"Well that might be of great help indeed," Watson responded hopefully. "What is the address?"

Cooper hesitated. He scratched his head. He stood up and paced a bit around the cell. Then he sat down again.

"I can't recall it, Dr. Watson. I'm sorry, but I can't remember the name of the street or the number. Dammit."

"What if..." Watson continued, "You were let out of this cell, Mr. Cooper? Do you think you would be able to show me how to get to the place, even if you couldn't remember the name of the street?"

Cooper nodded with an aura of certainty.

"Yes, Sir, I think I could. Do you really think the police would allow that? I think they are still considering whether or not to charge me with a crime."

"I shall see what I can do," said Watson. "Inspector Lestrade, come and let me out of here. There are things that you and I must discuss. Mr. Cooper, I promise to return shortly."

"Watson, surely you're not serious!" shouted Lestrade as soon as he and Watson were out of earshot of Edwin Cooper. "I can't just let you walk out of here with that man in your custody! He assaulted a handful of police officers. My superiors would have my head on a silver platter!"

"But, Inspector," Watson insisted, "this man's knowledge of the location of this place is vital to Seward's and my continuation of this investigation. Remember, Lestrade, you just got all the credit for finding and shooting the new Jack the Ripper. The least you can do is use some of that newly golden reputation of yours to help us out with this. Think of all the times Holmes and I have come to your aid."

Twenty minutes later, Watson and Lestrade returned to within sight distance of Cooper's cell. Lestrade had left Watson alone for a few minutes while going to speak to his superiors about securing permission to take the prisoner out for a few hours, making assurances that it was necessary for the furthering of the case's progress. He had his permission, the condition being that Cooper was not to be let out of Lestrade's sight, not even for a moment.

The three men were soon exiting the station house, Cooper smiling, looking relieved as he breathed in his first breath of fresh air in days. Lestrade led them to one of the police department's horse-drawn carriages. He would drive them, choosing to involve as few people in the matter as possible until they could determine exactly what it was they were chasing after. With Lestrade at the reins and Watson and Cooper in the cab, the carriage began to move through the streets of London. They had agreed before beginning the trip that their first stop would be Seward's hospital where they would pick the young doctor up and take him along on the investigation.

Watson, Lestrade, and Cooper arrived at the hospital. Watson went in to fetch Seward, while Lestrade remained with Cooper, insisting that he keep an eye on the prisoner.

Watson found Seward in his office, hurriedly scribbling some notes. Seward looked up to see who had entered and began to speak excitedly.

"Watson, I've gotten through to Morse, at least partially. He recognizes himself as himself and not as that Baalzephon thing!"

"That's excellent news, Seward!" Watson said, and began to explain his own success in finding and bringing Cooper. "And I've managed to find our fifth member of the Hooded Man's little circle. Mr. Edwin Cooper's mind seems to be clear as day and he's offered to take us to the place where those shadowy meetings were held. He's outside with Lestrade as we speak. Are you coming with us?"

Seward put down his pen.

"Why don't you bring them in, Watson? I'm sure we could all use a bite to eat, and I think it might be interesting to have Cooper, if he's really as lucid as you say he is, interact with Morse. Perhaps that would be of help to us. I'd like to talk with Cooper a bit before we all go chasing after phantoms."

Watson agreed and went outside to summon Lestrade and Cooper.

Within half an hour, Watson, Seward, Lestrade, and Cooper sat down to eat together. Edwin Cooper, overjoyed to have been, at least temporarily, released from prison, proved to be a witty, intelligent dinner companion, relating stories and anecdotes from his career in the banking industry. Watson and Seward also took the opportunity to update Lestrade and Cooper on the events that had occurred with the Bird family, as well as with Cromwell and Morse. Some of the details of the Terence Hendricks occurrences were related as well, although some things, such as Seward's breaking into the murderer's house, were omitted from the conversation.

The afternoon meal took longer than expected, mostly due to the fact that the four men enjoyed the food and conversation and time ticked by without them realizing it. Soon, dusk was visible outside the windows and they began to discuss the possibility of postponing the next stage of the investigation until the morning. Cooper expressed worry that this would mean his having to return to his cell for the night, but Seward assured him, as well as Inspector Lestrade, that there was ample room with comfortable accommodations for them to spend the night at the hospital. Lestrade somewhat hesitantly agreed. Watson also decided to spend the night there. Now knowing that there would be no need to rush what was turning out to be an enjoyable early evening, Seward called for a round of drinks for himself and his companions.

At the Bird residence, the remainder of the day had been a quiet, mournful one. The news of Alexander Bird's death had spread quickly through the surrounding community and friends and acquaintances of the family came along in a steady stream to offer support. Mrs. Dorothea Bird was in the parlor, surrounded by those who had come. Clarice, who had had enough of the attention and sympathy, had gone upstairs to retire early for the night. Her relief at no longer being burdened by her unexpected musical gift had now given way to two very different feelings, her sadness at the loss of her father, and a feeling of giddy infatuation towards her recently acquired friend, Dr. John Seward. She mourned for her father, but also sat hoping that it would not be too long before she might see Dr. Seward again. Those conflicting sets of thoughts competing for her attention, Clarice got into her nightgown, extinguished the lamp, and slowly felt her weary mind and body shut down as sleep came for her.

Downstairs from Clarice's bedroom, the visitors continued to come and go. With so many people, some close friends and some the most casual of acquaintances, coming to see Mrs. Bird, the tall, thin man found it quite easy to slip into the house unnoticed. He made himself part of the group of concerned neighbors who were entering through the front door and went inside with them. As they headed into the parlor to visit the widow, the thin man slipped away from the crowd and crept up the staircase. He made his way down the hallway and quietly turned the knob of the door to the sleeping girl's room. The thin man was quite skilled in the arts of stealth and abduction. The chloroform was efficiently applied and the girl's slenderness made it easy for him to carry her out through one of the house's rarely used rear doors. To the waiting carriage, attended by one of his companions in his mysterious occupation, the thin man carried Clarice Bird and soon they were miles away from the girl's home, with her mother and guests completely unaware of what had transpired.

Eventually, the Bird residence quieted down. The visitors left and Mrs. Bird found herself exhausted. The weight of the day's events was heavy on her mind. She did not go upstairs to check on Clarice. She did not even bother to undress. She walked, as if in a trance, to her bedroom, sat down upon the bed, and fell into a deep sleep with little delay.

As the morning light streamed into the window of one of the guest bedrooms of Seward's hospital, Watson opened his eyes, yawned once, and stood up from the bed. He had slept well and the accommodations had proven to be quite comfortable. Within a short time, he found himself seated at morning tea with Seward, Lestrade, and Cooper and, this time, Sullivan. The cook was busy preparing a small breakfast for the men to consume before they set out to find the location of the Hooded Man's meetings. Soon, the food was served. As they began to eat, they all turned their heads at once, responding to the sound of a loud knocking upon the hospital's main entrance door. Sullivan excused himself from the table to rise and see who was pounding so loudly and frantically. Moments later, he reappeared, this time accompanied by a shaking, distraught Dorothea Bird.

"Dr. Watson, Dr. Seward, thank God I've found you both! They've taken her! Someone came in the night and took my poor Clarice!"

Seward stood immediately. He looked as if intense worry had suddenly been launched to the front of his thoughts.

Watson, on the other hand, remained calm. He stood and walked over to Mrs. Bird. He took her by the arm and led her to a chair.

"Mrs. Bird, please try to remain calm," he said reassuringly. "Sit down and tell us what has happened."

Sullivan poured a cup of tea for the woman as she related the tale of her waking up, ascending the stairs to see how her daughter was feeling, entering Clarice's bedroom and finding her gone. The worried mother had searched the house from top to bottom and found no trace of her daughter. She knew something had occurred based on the state of the unmade bed and the subconscious whispers of parental intuition. She had left her home immediately and gone to Baker Street where Mrs. Hudson had kindly suggested that she look for Watson at Seward's hospital. The wise old landlady had been correct in sending Mrs. Bird to the hospital and she now sat in the company of the men she had, over the past few days, learned to trust when it came to the matter of the strange events that had been assaulting her family.

"Please," she begged of Watson, Seward, and their three companions, "You must help me. Wherever Clarice has gone, she is not safe! I can't bear the thought of losing her too, not after what happened to Alexander!"

Seward responded to the worried woman's plea.

"Mrs. Bird, I promise you that we shall do everything within our powers to find your daughter, and to help her. I swear that we will!"

"Sullivan," he said to his chief orderly, "You will remain here with Mrs. Bird. See that she has anything she needs. Watson, Lestrade, Cooper, I suggest we be on our way. We must find the place where those clandestine gatherings took place. The matter has now become many times more urgent than it was previously!"

With that, the four men marched out the door. Watson and Seward climbed into the cab of the horse-drawn carriage. Lestrade climbed atop the vehicle and took the reigns while Edwin Cooper sat beside him.

Chapter VII:
Under London, Out of London

Clarice Bird shivered as she awoke. She tried to move, but she struggled in vain. The room was mostly dark, but a small lamp in one corner provided enough light for Clarice to see something of the place where she was held. She was bound to a chair in a seated position, clad in the nightgown she had worn to bed. The stone floor was cold under her bare feet. She looked around as best as she could, to see that the room's floor and walls were of stone. There were no windows. The air had the musty, stale smell of a cellar, making Clarice assume that she was being held underground. She was afraid.

An eternity seemed to pass for Clarice. With no natural light being admitted to the room, she had no idea if it was day or night or how long she had been kept there. For what felt like hours, nothing happened. She heard no sounds, saw nothing but the lamp-lit interior of her stony, cold prison.

Finally, the thick-looking wooden door of the room let out a creaking sound. Clarice jumped a bit in her chair, startled, the fear running to the forefront of her mind as she wondered who would be revealed when the door had opened.

A man entered the room and closed the door behind him. He was clad in a long robe and his face was concealed by the shadows cast by his hood. Clarice gasped. The man drew back his hood, revealing a bald head and a face punctuated by two piercingly intense dark eyes. He smiled, but it was a twisted grin, a smile accented with a touch of madness boiling just beneath the surface of his expression.

"Hello, Clarice," the Hooded Man said. "I know you're wondering why you

have been brought here. The answer is truly quite simple. I want answers...
and the one who employs my services wants answers. You, my dear girl,
were exposed to a substance that has been shown to have certain very
interesting effects upon the mind. Those effects were apparent in your
behavior when you suddenly emerged as a musician of considerable talent.
Then, just as swiftly, those gifts vanished and here you sit, a normal young
woman again, as if nothing unusual had ever happened to you. I want to
know why, my employer wants to know why, and we most certainly will
soon learn why!"

Clarice struggled for a moment against the ropes that held her immobile
in her seat. She winced in slight pain from the burning sensation as the
ropes bit into her wrists and ankles.

"Let me go!" she strongly begged.

"Shut your mouth, child!" the Hooded Man snapped at her. "You will
speak only when I ask you to speak, or I shall bind your mouth shut as I've
bound your limbs! I will ask the questions and you will answer them. We
shall not deviate from that arrangement. Is that understood?"

Clarice nodded to indicate her comprehension.

"Good," continued the Hooded Man. "Tell me, child, when your mind
shifted its configuration, when you suddenly changed and were able to
play your unique brand of music, what did it feel like? Did you revel in it,
or was it an unpleasant thing?"

"I hated it!" Clarice answered, with the venom of harsh honesty in her
voice. "I became someone else, a person I did not even recognize as me!
If you were responsible for that, I hope you rot in Hell! If my father were
alive, he'd beat you senseless!"

The Hooded Man just laughed.

"My dear Miss Bird, your father was to blame for your condition."

Clarice spat at him, hitting him in the face. The Hooded Man took
three steps forward and slapped her across the face. She whimpered in
pain and tears began to run down her cheeks. The Hooded Man drew
his hand back and made ready to swing it forward to strike her again but,
mercifully for Clarice, a knock sounded on the other side of the room's
door. The Hooded Man aborted the motion of his hand, held his finger up
to his lips in a gesture meant to tell Clarice to keep silent, and turned to
answer the knocking.

He opened the door and the tall, thin man walked in. He was carrying
a medium sized leather satchel. He looked at Clarice for a moment. She
just stared back at both of her captors, not saying a word. The thin man
finally spoke.

"The man drew back his hood, revealing a bald head..."

"She wants to see the girl. I am to bring her to her at once. You will remain here."

The Hooded Man began to argue.

"But I was looking forward to the experience of interrogating the girl! What am I to do here?"

"You will be needed here," the thin man assured the Hooded Man. "You shall soon have visitors. Those two interfering physicians have contacted Edwin Cooper and convinced the police to release him. He will doubtlessly lead them here. You will stand ready to deal with them. Those are her orders."

The Hooded Man nodded as if he knew it was pointless to further argue the matter. The thin man walked over to Clarice and dropped his leather bag on the floor. He knelt and opened it. He drew a large, sharp knife from the bag. Clarice's eyes grew wide with terror and she gasped when she saw the blade. The thin man laughed.

"Don't worry, girl. This is not to be used on you…at least now."

He used the knife to cut the ropes that bound her.

"You can move now, but do not try anything! If you do, I will be using this knife! Here, put these on."

He pulled some clothes from the leather bag and handed them to her. She quickly pulled on the clothing, which was made for a small sized man, on over her nightgown. The shirt, trousers and shoes were uncomfortable and unlike the clothing she was used to, but being covered made her feel at least a bit less vulnerable.

The thin man led her from the room and down a long, dark corridor. After they walked for a minute, he stopped her and blindfolded her. They walked more. She could hear a door swing open and feel a breeze on her skin. The blindfold obscured her vision, but she could still see that the light had brightened and she knew they had gone outside. The thin man held onto her arm and helped her into a carriage. She sat in the cab and felt the vehicle begin to move. The thin man did not release his grip on her as they traveled.

The four investigators raced through the London streets. Lestrade drove, urging the horses on as Edwin Cooper navigated, directing Lestrade to turn the carriage left or right, north, south, east or west. He was navigating by visual memory rather than by any recollection of street names. In the carriage's cab, Seward and Watson sat and watched the scenery go by, the streets beginning to fill with other carriages and pedestrians as the morning hours went by and London woke up for the day. All four men were anxious to find the place they sought. They were all armed with revolvers except for Cooper, whom Lestrade would not allow to have a weapon as he was still a suspect in police custody. Lestrade was adamant about solving the case, as was Watson. Cooper wanted to put a stop to the chain of events that had landed him in a police cell to begin with. For Seward, the case had suddenly become more personal than it had been before. His growing feelings for the young Miss Clarice Bird were at the forefront of his mind and he was deeply concerned about her safety.

"You're thinking about the young lady, aren't you Seward?" Watson asked as they rode.

"Is it that obvious?" Seward asked back.

"Only to me I would think," said Watson. "I found myself in a similar situation once, during one of my earliest exploits with Sherlock Holmes."

"How did that work out for you?" Seward inquired, his curiosity aroused.

Watson took in a deep breath and answered.

"I married her. We were very happy for several years...until she died."

The carriage rattled on rapidly for a while longer. Watson and Seward watched from inside as it twisted and turned through London's streets. Finally, they came to a halt in front of a rather ordinary looking building. It appeared fairly normal on the outside. It was a building of several floors, brick walled and in good repair. It could have contained apartments or offices; there was nothing specific about it at all.

Seward and Watson got out of the carriage's cab as Lestrade and Cooper got down from the driver's perch.

"This is it, this is the right place!" Cooper said excitedly, pointing at the front door of the building. Lestrade walked over and tried the front door. It was unlocked.

"I'll go in first," said the inspector. "Cooper, I want you next after me so you can direct me on which way to go. Watson, Seward, you two will follow close behind and have your hands near your revolvers at all times. We don't know what, or who, we might find in there."

Lestrade drew his pistol and opened the door. The four men found themselves in a long hallway with doors on both sides, all of them closed.

"Which way now, Cooper?" Lestrade demanded.

"To the end of the corridor," was Edwin Cooper's reply. "I don't know what's behind these doors, but we need to go down the stairs and into the cellar. That's where we met with the Hooded Man."

They all proceeded down the hallway and found, as promised by Cooper, a staircase descending downwards. An oil lamp sat at the top of the stairs, apparently left there by whoever had been the last to come up from the lower level. Lestrade picked it up and lit it. He handed it to Cooper to carry because Cooper was the only one of the four who would not need his hands free to use a weapon if it were necessary to fight. Continuing on in the same walking order, they began to travel down the fairly long staircase.

At the bottom of the stairs, they found a single door. Lestrade pushed it open and they walked into a fairly large, unlit room with no windows or doors, except for the one through which they had entered. There was a table in the room, with six chairs around it.

"This is the room," said Cooper, "where our meetings were held. I would sit at the table with Bird and Cromwell and Morse and Terence…and we would wait for the Hooded Man to appear."

"You mean he would come through the door after the rest of you had arrived?" asked Lestrade.

"No," said Cooper. "He didn't come in through the door. He just came out of the shadows and he was here!"

"That's impossible!" Lestrade protested, clearly losing his patience. "Utter nonsense and rubbish!"

Watson, not wanting Lestrade and Cooper to begin to argue and distract the group from the purpose of their coming to that place, interjected.

"Gentlemen, please lower your voices. You may very well both be correct. When Seward and I spoke at length with Alexander Bird, he indicated that he suspected that a sort of hidden doorway might exist within this room, thus allowing the Hooded Man to create the illusion that he was appearing 'out of thin air.' I suggest that we examine the walls of this room for any section that might conceal such an entrance."

Seward, wishing to support Watson's words with actions, was the first to move towards one of the room's interior walls. He began to run his hands along the smooth stone surface of the wall, looking for any irregularity that might be a sign of something unusual. Within seconds, Lestrade and Cooper had put aside their disagreement and joined the search. They all worked their way along the walls for what seemed like much longer than it truly was. Their hands slid along the walls, searching for any irregularities in the apparent solidity of the stone. After many minutes had gone by, Seward felt a slight change in the surface of the section of wall that he was examining.

"Over here!" he called out to his companions.

The others rushed over. Cooper held up the lamp, shining the yellowish glow upon the wall. Just barely noticeable, they could see a seam where a door, tightly closed with no visible handle or knob, was hidden in the wall.

"Here it is," Seward said, "but how do we open it? There's no knob and the line of the seam is too narrow to even attempt to pry it open. Perhaps it can only be opened from the other side."

"Let me see it," said Lestrade, and rather rudely pushed his way past Seward and Cooper to get to the door. He raised his hand and began to knock on the door in an oddly rhythmic manner, tapping out a pattern of sorts.

After about twenty of those taps on the door, Watson, Seward and Cooper gasped in surprise as the door made an odd creaking noise and slid open, Lestrade's tapping having activated some sort of mechanism!

"How the devil did you manage that, Lestrade?" asked Watson, shocked.

"Just a hunch," answered the inspector. "I'm as surprised as you are that it worked. All this mumbo jumbo about hooded men and such made me think of my days as a Freemason. I joined a lodge as a youngster, but haven't bothered to go to the meetings in years now. I recalled a special knock used in one of the old ceremonies, and I decided to try it out. I didn't think it would work!"

Lestrade marched through the now open doorway. The others followed in the order they had thus far used; Cooper and his lamp, then Watson, and Seward last. They went through the doorway and into a new hallway, this one narrower and colder than the previous.

They continued walking as the hallway seemed to stretch out for a long way ahead of them. Their view of what lay ahead was limited to the distance illuminated by the glow of Cooper's lamp. Then, up ahead, another speck of light appeared, the glow of a separate lamp! The four investigators quickened their pace, walking faster, but not running, for fear of tripping in the still dimly lit space. As they moved forward, the light ahead seemed to come towards them as well. Finally, the four of them met the possessor of the other lamp. There, in that dark, subterranean corridor, the four investigators came face to face with the Hooded Man.

"It's him!" shouted Cooper.

The Hooded Man stopped and glared at them. His face was darkened by shadows cast by his hood. He held the lamp in one hand and raised the other hand to remove his hood. When the hood was down, it became apparent that he was wearing a scarf over the lower half of his face, covering his nose and mouth. Seward, putting two and two together in his mind, realized why the Hooded Man might cover his face so.

"Watch out!" Seward shouted. The Hooded Man reached into his robe and quickly pulled his hand out again, thrusting it towards those he had just met and flinging a handful of powder at them!

Watson had caught on to what was happening as soon as Seward had shouted. He grabbed hold of Lestrade and pulled him back out of the way of the shower of dust. Watson and Lestrade toppled backwards, bowling over Seward, landing the three of them in a heap on the stone floor. They landed with a thud, but managed to avoid the cloud of powder, or at least most of it. Edwin Cooper was not so fortunate. He was hit full in the face by the Hooded Man's attack and inhaled a lungful of the dust. He began to scream as the effects of the dust unhinged his mind.

"The land is melting and I must go!" he shouted.

The Hooded Man turned and ran down the hallway, back in the direction from which he had come. The powder had mostly rained down now and was settling, harmlessly, on the floor. Watson, Seward and Lestrade untangled themselves and got to their feet. Cooper was growing madder by the second. He had, at least, the presence of mind to carefully put down the lamp, lest he toss it aside in his lunacy and shatter it. Lestrade took a step towards Cooper.

"Easy, Mr. Cooper, easy," Lestrade said, trying to calm him.

Cooper lunged at Lestrade. Before the inspector could stop him, before Seward or Watson could interfere, Cooper grabbed the revolver from Lestrade's hand, put it to his own temple, and fired! He fell to the floor, dead, another fatality of the Hooded Man's powder of madness.

Mere seconds had gone by since the initial scattering of the powder. The Hooded Man's footsteps could still be heard down the hallway. Watson pointed his revolver straight ahead and slightly downward and fired down the dark corridor.

"Aaargh!" echoed a cry of pain from up ahead. Stepping over the corpse of Cooper and taking care not to slip on the pooling blood, Watson, Lestrade and Seward raced to the place from where the scream had come.

A hundred feet ahead lay the Hooded Man, bleeding from a wound to the leg. Watson's aim had been true, felling the villain but not killing him. They stopped and knelt down. Watson took out a handkerchief and set to work stopping the bleeding. Lestrade was about to question the groaning Hooded Man, but Seward took the initiative first. He grabbed the Hooded Man by the collar of his robe and shook him roughly.

"Where is Clarice Bird?" Seward growled threateningly. "What have you done with her?"

The Hooded Man said nothing; he just stared back at Seward. Seward shook him again. Watson held his hand up in a signal for Seward to stop.

"Easy, Seward, he's losing blood. Don't forget, you're a doctor!"

Seward shot right back at Watson, his anger and concern getting the better of him.

"Dammit, Watson, I'm not worried about the Hippocratic Oath at the moment. I'm worried about Clarice!"

He slammed his hand down on the Hooded Man's wounded leg, causing the injured man to howl and tremble in agony.

"Does it hurt? Good, you filthy beast! Now where is she?"

The Hooded Man's eyes filled with tears. He whimpered and then he spoke.

"Stop, stop. I'll tell you where she is…but you won't be able to help her…"

"Then speak!" Seward shouted at him. Watson stood ready to interfere if Seward tried to exert force again, while Lestrade stood watching, curious to see what Seward would do next if he did not like the Hooded Man's answer.

The Hooded Man spoke.

"Kellington…Kellington Manor…" and then he fainted.

Watson checked the Hooded Man's pulse with his fingers.

"He's alive, just fainted, probably from loss of blood and the intense pain. He said 'Kellington Manor.' Have either of you heard of such a place?"

Seward and Lestrade both indicated ignorance of a place with such a name.

"Well then we'll have to learn what we can, and quickly," Watson continued. "Lestrade, take this man, this criminal, to a hospital. Once he's patched up, I'm sure you'll want to arrest him for the murder of Edwin Cooper. Seward, come with me!"

Not waiting for Lestrade or Seward to respond to his sudden flurry of barked orders, Watson headed back down the hallway, stepped over the body of Cooper, and went back up to the ground floor of the building. He waited upstairs and was soon joined by the others. Seward helped Lestrade to place the unconscious Hooded Man into the carriage. Lestrade drove off and Seward rejoined Watson. Watson was quite pleased with the way he had taken charge of the situation. At times like that one, he sometimes realized how much his time with Sherlock Holmes had influenced him.

"What now?" Seward asked.

"The library," Watson replied. "If this Kellington Manor is anywhere in or near London, we should be able to find information about it there."

Clarice finally felt the carriage come to a stop. The tall, thin man helped her out of the cab and removed her blindfold. She looked around as he led her away from the carriage. They were clearly outside the city streets of London. There were trees all around, woods. Up ahead was a very large building, a mansion that must have once been stunningly beautiful, but seemed to have fallen into a serious state of disrepair. The thin man was not forceful or rough with Clarice now; there was no reason for force. She had nowhere to run to and she knew it. He led her through the tree lined pathway towards the old mansion. They walked up to the front door and the thin man knocked in a pattern that Clarice assumed must have been planned in advance. A moment later, the door opened and a large man let them in. The man was different than anyone Clarice was used to seeing on the streets of London or any other English town. He was large, well over six feet tall and close to three-hundred and fifty pounds. His beard was full and thick. He was dressed in what Clarice assumed were the clothes of some kind of gypsy; he looked like pictures she had seen of nomadic people in the more Eastern portions of Europe. He did not say anything in English to her or the thin man. He simply grunted and motioned for them to enter. As they walked past the huge doorman, Clarice shivered when she noticed the large, curved knife hanging from the gypsy's belt.

The thin man led Clarice up the house's long, spiraling staircase. As they went up, she finally gathered the courage to speak.

"Why am I here? Where are you taking me now?"

"You will soon see," answered the thin man. "The one to whom I am loyal has asked to see you, and so here we are."

They reached the top of the stairs and entered a room. There was no door in the entrance of the room, just black curtains hanging down in the doorway, which parted in the middle when they went in. The interior of the room was dark, lit only by candles. The windows had been boarded up. The thin man and Clarice stopped in the middle of the room. No one else seemed to be there. For a moment, it crossed Clarice's mind that perhaps this man had brought her here to assault her, but that terrible thought was dispelled by a voice suddenly coming from the shadowy edges of the room.

"You may go now. Leave the girl here," said a voice that sounded so brittle and old that Clarice trembled at its sound, wondering if it had come from a human being, or a ghost.

The thin man walked out the way he had come in, leaving Clarice standing alone in the middle of the room, wondering what would happen next. Her mind was spinning. Only days before, she had been living the normal life of a typical young woman in London but, suddenly, she had been through a series of twists and turns; the piano playing, her father's sudden suicide, the loss of the piano playing, the appearance of the handsome doctor whom she now felt so drawn to, and now she had been kidnapped!

The figure to which the ancient sounding voice belonged now came walking out of the shadows, becoming visible to Clarice.

Clarice could not help but gasp. It was a woman, or so Clarice thought. It wore a long red dress that would have looked regal and impressive on any other person, but there was no garment in the world that would have made this woman's appearance any less shocking. She was old, older than anyone Clarice had ever seen before, but moved with a certain strength and speed that should have belonged to a younger woman. She had long, flowing hair of absolutely pure white, as if it had grown in a time when color had not yet come into the universe. The face was etched with wrinkles and lines deeper than any Clarice had ever seen. The eyes were dark, deep and terribly intense. Her hands were long-fingered, as wrinkled and bent as the rest of her, and ended in long, talon-like nails. She looked decrepit and aged to a disturbing degree. Clarice just stared, wide-eyed and afraid.

"Hello, child," said the withered crone, with a voice tinted with an accent that sounded to Clarice like it originated in some Eastern European nation. Perhaps she was related to the massive male gypsy who had opened the door for the thin man, thought Clarice.

"Who are you?" asked the frightened young girl.

The old hag laughed.

"I will not tell you my name. I will assume that you would know it, but were I too speak it; you might die of pure fright! Let me pay you a compliment though, child. You radiate youth and beauty. There was a time when I would have used that youthful vitality and made it my own! Was this another place and time, you would be put to a much useful death for my benefit!" said the crone, walking several steps closer to Clarice.

As she walked towards the terrified girl, the old woman thought back upon her life, her very long life. Though any sane person might not have believed it, she was well over three hundred years old! She had been born in Hungary in the year 1560, into a family of royalty and had born the title and name of Countess Elizabeth Bathory. She had discovered that amazing healing and regenerative properties could be found in the blood of young women and had, for years, lured such women to her castle and mercilessly and brutally slain them to satisfy her addiction to bathing in blood in an attempt to preserve her own youth. When what she had been doing was discovered, she was sealed inside a bricked-in room until she died, or at least that is what people were told. In truth, she had escaped her prison and fled from Hungary. She traveled throughout Europe searching for means to stave off the advancing of age. She had come across certain arcane means of doing so, but something had gone wrong. She had managed to greatly extend her lifetime, but had continued to age! Now, she was an ancient wrinkled thing, a grotesque parody of the porcelain-skinned beauty she once had been, but she had not died. She did not feel three centuries old, but she looked it!

Her mind snapped back to her present and she reached out her twisted hand, longing to touch the soft, supple flesh of Clarice's face. As she reached out to the girl, she could hear the footsteps of another person entering the room.

"Elizabeth, do not touch that child! She has been brought here at my request, not for your sick amusements!" called out the new arrival. It was the voice of a woman.

Elizabeth Bathory turned to the doorway. Rage was in her eyes.

"I have told you repeatedly not to address me so casually! I am royalty!"

"No," said the woman. "You once were royalty. Now you answer to me. Do not forget that it is I who have supported you in recent times, taking you in because we are alike in many ways, when no one else will have you, you horrid and deformed wretch! You will not see the blood of this girl today. You will do as you are told. Now leave us!"

The creature that had once been known as the dreaded Blood Countess did as she was ordered and left the room. Clarice Bird turned her gaze to the woman who had commanded the crone to depart.

This woman was far younger than the one who had just left the room. She was, Clarice estimated, in her middle or late thirties. Her voice sounded American, with a hint of an attempt to sound British.

"Sit down, Miss Bird," the woman said. "We must talk."

Watson and Seward had left the building where they had encountered and injured the Hooded Man and raced to the nearest library. They made quick use of the library's maps and information about the city of London and its surrounding areas, quickly finding what they so desperately sought.

Kellington Manor was a large, expensively designed residence several miles outside the perimeter of the city. It had been erected nearly one hundred and fifty years earlier, but had since fallen into disuse and was classified as "abandoned" in the official records. After reading that small bit of information on the manor, Seward located it on the map and he and Watson raced out of the library and back onto the streets. They rented two horses, assuming they could travel more quickly that way than in a hansom carriage. Mounted upon their hired steeds, they rode as quickly as they could towards the area pinpointed on the library's map. Their journey took them beyond the officially recognized borders of London and into the wooded areas, punctuated by twisting, unpaved roadways, which surrounded the great city. They rode on for nearly two hours, stopping for nothing until; finally, the worn stone shell of Kellington Manor appeared ahead of them.

They halted their horses a half mile from the manor and secured them by rope to two trees. They dismounted and began to walk towards the towering structure. Both doctors instinctively felt inside their coats to be certain that their revolvers were ready should they need them, as they both had reason to expect to. Watson was fairly calm, having become somewhat used to marching towards danger during both his military days and his adventures with Sherlock Holmes. Seward was not afraid. His desire to find and aid Clarice Bird overwhelmed any fear that might have otherwise affected him. Onward they walked, unsure of what lay ahead of them.

Chapter VIII:
Clouds of Hate and Vengeance

"I spent several very interesting months in the Orient," said the woman to Clarice. "I went there in search of secrets, of power, of the means to make myself into something more than just another mere woman of the Western world. It was there that I found a certain substance, a powder of such fascinating effect that it could knock down the barriers of men's minds… or women's minds for that matter, unlocking hidden desires and ways of behavior that were otherwise buried deeply beneath the fortresses erected by so-called 'society.' I thought that this powder would be the means by which I would make myself immortal, not of body, but of reputation, becoming someone whom the entire world would remember for a very long time. Then I continued my travels and I had certain experiences that led me to change the course of my actions. I went from seeking great power to seeking great revenge. The target of my vengeance was not an individual human being, but an entire society, a population. I wanted to destroy the whole of London. I will soon accomplish that goal. London will go down a terrible road; first a road of madness, and then a road of destruction. Murder and suicide will come with great fire…and London will die!"

Clarice gasped. The words she was hearing come from this woman's lips could not be the words of a sane person. Surely her captor must have been crazed!

"Let me go!" Clarice shouted. "Let me go!"

The woman paced the room as she spoke; Clarice stood completely still. She was terrified.

"Why?" the girl asked. "What has London done to cause you to hate it so?"

Half a mile from the interior of Kellington Manor, John Watson and John Seward had begun to jog at a fairly brisk pace towards the large mansion ahead of them. The distance began to rapidly close between the two doctors and their destination. When they had come to within several hundred feet of the front of Kellington Manor, Watson stopped and stood against the back of a tree to conceal him. Seward, following Watson's lead, paused as well and knelt down to avoid being seen by anyone who might be looking out from the manor's high windows.

"We must approach with stealth now, Seward. We have no way of knowing what dangers might await us as we near that place," said Watson.

Seward nodded. He was not a complete stranger to perilous circumstances himself, having been in several nearly deadly incidents during the dreadful affair with the Transylvanian count, Dracula. Being the younger of the two men, Seward heeded Watson's words, respecting the older doctor's experience. Watson, Seward knew, had no knowledge of the Dracula situation. Seward had not spoken of it, for fear that Watson would find the admittedly far-fetched tale hard to swallow and think Seward less than sane.

"We cannot very well go knocking on the front door," Watson decided. "We should work our way, quietly and cautiously, around to the back of the building. You go around on the left side and I shall go to the right. If we both manage to reach the rear of the house without incident, I will meet you in the back."

Seward nodded once again to indicate that he understood Watson's plan. The two men separated and snuck through the trees and brush on either side of the property until they were each bordering their respective sides of the large manor. Both were prepared for danger should it rear its head, both had one hand ready to draw their weapon should it become necessary to do so.

Seward crept as quietly as he could along the left wall of the mansion. He saw no signs of human activity. It was now late in the afternoon and the sun was beginning to set, but there was still sufficient light to clearly see his surroundings.

On the other side of Kellington Manor, Watson too kept a steady pace towards the back of the building. He darted in and out of the convenient cover of trees, bushes and shrubbery, trying to keep out of sight as much as possible as he moved on his way to meet Seward at the rear wall.

Watson had thought he was alone, thought he was keeping out of sight, but he suddenly heard a word shouted out in a language he did not understand, shouted in a heavily accented voice. He turned quickly and saw a large man, clad in a disheveled coat and loose trousers running at him, holding a large knife. Behind the suddenly approaching man were two others, similarly dressed, one thin and wiry and the other of more average build. Watson knew he had been spotted. He had no desire to hurt anyone until he was certain they were foes and he knew that he would have time to fire only one shot before his pursuers were upon him. He knew he was in a position in which he could be easily captured, and hoped that capture was all that was on the minds of those men, not something deadlier. He decided that warning Seward was the wise thing to do. He took out his revolver and fired once, into the air.

There was no time for a second shot. The largest of the three pursuers leaped and tackled him. Watson felt his body slam into the ground, knocking the wind out of him. He felt a large, powerful fist slam into the side of his head and he fell unconscious.

The large man lifted Watson's limp body with ease. His two companions caught up with him and the three began to walk towards the back of the house with their unconscious captive. The medium sized man took the revolver that Watson had dropped when tackled and put it into his own pocket.

Seward, on the left side of Kellington Manor, heard the sound of the gunshot and began to move more quickly to the rear of the building. To Hell with staying out of sight now, he thought to himself; Watson may be in danger!

He turned the corner and had a clear line of sight across the back of the manor and was able to see the three men, dressed like Eastern European gypsies entering the manor by way of the rear entrance. Seward knew their type. They were gypsies of the Carpathian Mountains; the type of men who had served Dracula and who Seward had held off at gunpoint as Harker and Morris had slain their terrible, vampiric foe! The big one was carrying Watson. Seward, not usually a religious man, found himself praying that his friend was only unconscious, and not dead.

When the door had closed behind the gypsies, Seward snuck up to it. There was a small window, which he looked into. He could see only darkness.

On one of the upper floors of Kellington Manor, Clarice Bird and the woman who had become her host both instinctively turned their heads at the sound of the gunshot that seemed to have come from outside the manor. They could, of course, see nothing, for the room which they occupied had been rendered windowless, large boards of wood nailed over the walls' openings to block out all light. The woman shrugged and turned back to the captive girl.

"What has London done to ignite my hatred, you ask? It had done enough. That is all I will say. The powder I possess will help me to destroy it. You, however, remain a mystery to me. Somehow, you have overcome the effects of my dusty weapon. I have brought you here to test it on you once again, in hopes that your apparent resistance to the powder's powers can be overcome by a larger, second dose. It shall be no accidental exposure this time, child! You will feel the full potency of this wondrous weapon which only I, in all of Europe, can lay claim to!"

As the woman gloated, the tall, thin man entered the room.

"What is it, Percival?" the woman asked, sounding annoyed. "I am occupied with my young guest!"

"I beg your pardon, Mistress," said Percival sheepishly. "Your gypsy servants have captured a man attempting to sneak into the building. It is one of the men who have been investigating our activities, the older of the two doctors. They have him downstairs. He will soon regain consciousness. Do you wish us to kill him?"

The woman shook her head.

"No, Percival. Let him live for now. I want you and one of the gypsies to bring him here to me. That one is an old acquaintance of mine. Take this girl and place her in Elizabeth's care for now, and then bring me Dr. Watson!"

Percival bowed to the woman who commanded him. He took hold of Clarice's arm and led her from the room. She did not resist as she knew that flight was not an intelligent option at this point. If Watson was inside the manor already, she knew, there was a chance that Seward might be nearby. She hoped and prayed that he would come and help her.

After Percival had removed the girl from her sight, the woman sat down on one of the candlelit room's small couches and waited.

On the ground floor of the manor, Watson woke up. His head and body ached but he felt all right for a man who had just been tackled by a giant of a man and then knocked unconscious with a blow to the head. He blinked twice, took in a beep breath, flexed his aching limbs and looked around the room. The three gypsies stood watching him. Another man entered the room. This one was tall and thin, with a sly, predatory look to his face.

"Hello, Dr. Watson," said Percival. "There is someone within this house who wishes to visit with you immediately. You will come with me. Gregor, keep a hand on the good doctor."

The largest of the three gypsies, the one who had tackled Watson outside, grunted in affirmation of Percival's orders. He grabbed Watson roughly by the arm and forced him to stand. Percival went up the house's long staircase first, followed by Watson and Gregor.

Outside the rear door of the house, Seward looked for a way in that would not involve any risk of attracting attention to him. He could find none. He decided to take a risk, hoping that the group of men who had dragged Watson inside had left the area near the door and was now out of earshot. He remembered the steps he had taken to break into the home of Terence Hendricks. He removed his jacket, wrapped it around his forearm to prevent himself from being cut, and smashed the window. Avoiding the remaining shards of glass, he reached in and unlocked the door. The latch released and he turned the exterior knob. He pulled the door open and went inside. It was growing dark now and he had to squint slightly to see in the dusky inside of the manor. He slipped through the backrooms and into the main hallway of the ground floor. He found a long staircase going upwards and a second staircase descending down into whatever chambers existed below the house, under the ground. He considered his next move for a moment, deciding to take the lower route first. He took out his revolver, holding it at the ready, and began to creep down the stairs.

In a dark, dingy basement chamber, below the main floor of Kellington Manor, Clarice Bird sat in an old, wooden rocking chair, breathing in the decrepit underground air and trembling slightly, half from the chill of the approaching night, and half from fear. In front of her, the aged and prune-faced form of the woman called Elizabeth Bathory paced back and forth, her dark and malicious eyes gleaming in the pale candlelight.

"Time is an old friend of mine, girl," said the demented old crone. "For centuries, I have been witness to its passage. I understand it, and it often benefits me. I am going to tell you something about time. For you, it is growing shorter and shorter. With my patience, time runs out. To a certain extent, I follow the wishes of the woman I left you with earlier, but there is a limit to my patience. If she does not send for you soon, I shall claim you as my own, and you shall help me to once again perform the dark rites that have given me some semblance of immortality!"

Seward reached the bottom of the stairs. There was only a small landing where he now stood. In front of him was a thick and sturdy looking wooden door. There was no window and the door was closed tight. It made him uneasy to realize that there was no chance of previewing what awaited him behind that door. He gathered his courage, thought of the danger that might be confronting Clarice and Watson at that very moment, and he pushed the door open. He stepped through the threshold, revolver at the ready, and looked around.

The room was lit by wall-mounted torches and there were two men inside, two of the gypsies from earlier! They whirled around at the sound of the opening door. One held a dagger and the other had a pistol. Seward fired his revolver at the one with the gun. He surprised himself with the accuracy of his aim. He had struck the gypsy square in the chest and watched as he fell forward, apparently dead!

The dagger wielder advanced. Seward fired again. The bullet struck the gypsy's shoulder, causing a howl of pain, but not stopping him. He tried to pounce, the gleaming dagger flashing towards Seward's throat, but Seward's third shot rang out and shattered the gypsy's skull. Death was immediate. Seward did not wait for the sound of his three shots to draw attention from anyone who might have heard them. He picked up the gun that the first gypsy had dropped upon his death. He recognized it as Watson's revolver and put it in his pocket. He assumed that it still contained four bullets, as Watson has used one to shoot the Hooded Man and Seward had not seen him reload. A second bullet was discharged outside the house when Watson had been ambushed. Seward mentally noted that his own weapon still held three rounds, which left a total of seven bullets at his disposal. He went through the next door that he saw and found a long hallway, similar to the one in which he and his companions had encountered the Hooded Man under London. This hallway, like the room he had just left, was illuminated by hanging torches. Up ahead, he could see a door like the one he had just entered through. He raced in the direction of that door.

"The dagger wielder advanced. Seward fired again."

He reached the door and kicked it open. Behind the door was a dimly lit chamber with stone walls. Straight ahead, he saw the small, fragile, shivering form of Clarice Bird. She looked unharmed, but was shaking, clad in ill-fitting men's clothing.

"Clarice!" he exclaimed as he stepped into the room, wanting to embrace her.

She screamed.

"John, watch out!"

With an evil howl, like the voice of a harpy from out of the deepest bowels of Hell, Elizabeth Bathory emerged from the shadowy corner and slashed at him with a silver knife. The blade sliced into his forearm, drawing blood and sending agony through his nerves. He involuntarily released his grip on his revolver and it clattered to the stony floor. Bathory raised the knife for another slash, but Seward dodged. He fell backwards onto the floor and swept outwards with his leg. Bathory tripped, stumbling backwards. She let go of her knife, but regained her standing position with a speed and agility that seemed unnatural for a woman who looked as old and almost mummified as she did. She thrust her long, twisted, claw-like fingers out in front of her and charged at Seward, seemingly intent on clawing out his eyes. He had just enough time to reach into his coat and draw out Watson's gun. He fired. The bullet slammed into the deranged countess's shoulder and knocked her backwards. She landed hard on her backside. Seward stood.

Clarice stood up as well. She did not run to Seward. Her face took on an expression of rage and fire. She picked up one of the two large, brass candleholders that lit the room. The candle fell out and landed on the floor, its flame extinguished on the hard stone surface. She walked over to where the countess had fallen and slammed the candlestick into the crone's head. She hit her again, and then again. Seward winced as he heard the splintering of aged, brittle bone.

"Die, you disgusting witch! Die!" shouted Clarice, malice and anger coloring her voice. Elizabeth Bathory, who had lived long ages and victimized myriad innocent people, died there, in a cold, musty subterranean chamber, several miles outside the borders of London, England.

Clarice ran to Seward. They embraced.

"I knew you'd come for me, John. I knew it," the young girl said, and then her tears of relief began to flow.

Seward tore a strip of cloth from the dead countess's dress and bound his wounded arm. He and Clarice began to walk back down the basement hallway. He had found one of the people he had sought. Now he had to locate Watson. He hoped he would not be too late.

High above, on the highest floor of Kellington Manor, Watson found himself standing outside a curtained doorway. Gregor still had a firm grip on his arm.

"You will enter and speak to the one who leads us," said Percival. We will be out here. Should you try to harm her or escape, Gregor and I will come in…and we will kill you!"

Gregor gave Watson a shove, not enough to knock him over, but enough to indicate that he should go through the curtains and learn who or what awaited his company inside the room.

Watson entered the room and heard the curtains close behind him. The room was dark, lit only by candles. Across the room, Watson could see someone; a woman, to judge by the silhouette of her body, clothing, and long, flowing hair, he observed. Then she spoke, and her voice sent chills through Watson's minds and body, chills that went as deep as his bones, for he knew that voice and it brought an intense rush of memories and images to his startled mind.

"Hello, Watson," said the woman's voice. "It is a pleasure to see you again."

Watson, could he have seen himself, would have noted that he had suddenly gone pale, so unexpected was the identity of this woman. He spat out the first words he could manage.

"Irene Adler! Good Lord!"

Watson's mind flashed back in time to one of his earliest cases with Sherlock Holmes. Irene Adler had been a brilliantly talented singer, performing all over Europe. She had been born in the United States but had found her greatest success on the Continent. She had retired from the opera in her late twenties. Coming to London, she had become embroiled in a somewhat scandalous affair with a member of one of Europe's royal families. It was as a result of this series of events that she came into contact with Sherlock Holmes, thus becoming the only person whom Watson had ever seen outsmart the great detective. After the conclusion of the case, Adler had gone off to marry a man called Godfrey Norton. Holmes had never seen her again, but held her in the highest possible esteem. A photograph of Miss Adler had become one of Holmes' most prized possessions. Watson had not seen her again either, until this moment.

"You look surprised to see me, my good doctor," she said with a sly, confident smile.

"You're the one behind all this madness and misery?" Watson begged her for an answer. "Why? Why would you involve yourself in such matters? You earned our respect, that of Holmes and me! This is most disappointing, Miss Adler...or Mrs. Norton, whichever name you carry now!"

"Doctor Watson, you and your companion also earned my greatest respect and, in fact, it relieved me greatly to learn that Holmes had temporarily left London, for he shall now be spared the fate of the rest of this city. You, my physician friend, will not be so fortunate, I fear. If you will give me a few moments, I shall explain these matters to you. Will you indulge me with a bit of patience? "

"I don't seem to have much of a choice in the matter, do I?" asked Watson with supreme sarcasm.

Adler sat down and motioned for Watson to do the same.

"The last you saw of me, I had gone off to marry one Godfrey Norton, and I did so. The marriage was a joy in its very beginnings, but I quickly grew to learn one vital fact. The man I had married was...a bore! I could tolerate it no longer, his normalcy, his banality, his simple-minded habits and the drudgery of daily life as his wife. So I left him, left him one night after he had gone to bed. I took a fairly large sum of money from our shared purse and stole away in the darkness. I did not know where I should go, but I began to travel about Europe in search of knowledge, in search of excitement, in search of adventure. Anything would have suited me better than life as a simple, average woman! As I traveled, I heard whispers of many things esoteric, ways of acquiring strange powers, means of controlling others, ways of becoming more than just a mere mortal. Although I suspected that most such things were mere superstition, I must confess that such ideas held great appeal for me.

"Eventually, my travels took me to the dark sections of Eastern Europe, in the vicinity of the Carpathian Mountains. It was there that I heard hushed rumors of a man, or something more than a man, a being who held those who lived nearby in a grip of terror and fear. No one would tell me exactly what manner of being he supposedly was, but temptation got the better of me and I vowed to find a way to meet this mysterious man face to face. I tried to pay for transport to his home, a place spoken of in whispers as Castle Dracula. No matter how much money I offered to the peasant folk, it was not enough to counteract the sheer terror that any mention of that castle evoked in them.

"Finally, I decided to take matters into my own hands and make the journey myself. I purchased a horse and rode by day, stopping only when those mountain regions grew dark with night, stopping only to sleep a few short hours before resuming my travels. As I neared the dreaded abode of this ill-spoken of count, the horse grew more skittish. One morning I woke to find that it had chewed through the rope that bound it to a tree and fled altogether. I would not give up my quest to reach Castle Dracula. I walked the last few days. Finally, exhausted, nearly starved, my mind and body on the brink of collapse, I reached my destination!

"Much to my surprise, the count himself opened the door when I pounded upon it. I must have fainted when I first saw him, probably from sheer exhaustion, for I awoke three days later. I found myself in bed in one of the high towers of the great castle. I was clad in a gown of the most luxurious silk, a gown that looked and felt like something out of a child's fairy story. The inhabitant of the castle had tended to me, administered care that broke the fever that had nearly killed me after my tiredness must have made me susceptible to its fury. He had bandaged my feet, which had been torn to shreds by the long, grueling walk in shoes unfit for such an ordeal.

"For nearly a month I remained at the castle. My host was a strange man, unlike any I had ever encountered before. He looked ancient, but had the spirit and vitality of a man decades younger. He projected supreme confidence and power. His habits were odd. He would often vanish into the deep, dark corridors of the castle during the daylight hours and reemerge when dusk arrived, sitting and talking with me as I dined, but I don't recall ever seeing him eat any food at all. His presence was of the type that I have always been drawn to and I must confess to you, Dr. Watson, that his quiet confidence, his deeply intellectual nature, and his hawk-like expression reminded me strongly of Mr. Sherlock Holmes!

"It was clear to me how his ways could be frightening to the simple-minded, superstitious peasants of the surrounding villages, but I liked the man and I grew to feel quite comfortable there in his presence. For most of my stay, I saw no one else, save for the gypsies who would sometimes arrive just after nightfall. Count Dracula would meet them by the castle's great front entranceway. There, the gypsies would linger for only moments as the count spoke to them in a language I did not speak, in a tone that made me think he was issuing commands or orders. The gypsies would nod and then rush off into the darkness of those mountains, as if hell-bent on accomplishing whatever it was that the count had sent them off to do. Once the gypsies had departed, the count would return to me and we would talk. He often related tales of the past to me, stories of days that had ended centuries ago, but in a manner of storytelling that made it seem as if he had witnessed the events with his own eyes. He was a fascinating man.

"After some time, the count told me that he would be leaving his home for a time. He apologized to me, but insisted that I leave Castle Dracula and continue my travels. I asked him if he would welcome me should I someday return to those mountains, but he did not reply at all, simply looking into the shadows as if his heart and mind had suddenly been thrown into the deep wells of his memories. He gave me some old, gold coins that were worth a small fortune and sent me off, handing me over to a small band of gypsies who drove me in their wagon back to a small town where I was able to board a train to continue my travels. That was the last I saw of Count Dracula.

"I went to Paris next, where I took a few of the gold coins to a dealer in antiquities. He nearly fainted when he saw them, and he paid me handsomely for them when he had recovered from the shock. I refused to tell him where I had acquired them. I now had a large sum of modern currency, as well as a handful of coins remaining. The money I had received in Paris was enough to book passage to the Orient.

"The Far East was like another world to me. I hired a guide, a well-traveled Englishman named Percival, whom you have already met. We were soon joined by another man, an expert in the occult customs of many regions. I believe you met him earlier today."

Watson nodded.

"Yes, I certainly did, if you refer to the bald man who wore a hooded robe. I shot him, but he still lives, albeit in the custody of the police."

Irene Adler just nodded and continued her narrative.

"Those two men were not the strongest minded of the male species. I soon became what in American slang might be called the 'Boss' of the three of us. Still, I was glad to have them along, for they served as translators and companions. In a certain desolate mountain region, we visited a monastery where we were fortunate enough to learn of a strange, secret substance, the powder with which I believe you were, for a short time, intimately familiar. The powers and properties of this substance were known to no native of the West until I found it. Suspecting that I would one day have a use for this powder, either for my own use or as a defense against some enemy I might make in my travels, I bought a generous supply of it from the monks. They did not mind parting with it, as I gave them more money than any of them had ever seen in their lives.

"I went on with my journeys, my two male companions traveling with me then. We went back in the direction of Europe. In Warsaw I found the next member of my little entourage, a strange, aged creature called Elizabeth who, like Count Dracula, held some of the darkest secrets of the eons in her twisted mind. Deciding that she might be of use to me someday, I took her with us. We continued on for another year, lacking nothing, for the gold I had been given was still plentiful.

"During that year, I had thought often of Dracula, and I had grown to miss him, such a great effect had our time together had on me. I made the decision to return to the Carpathian Mountains and see if he had returned to his castle. With my three companions along, I made the voyage there. On that occasion, the trip was made easier by the amount of wealth that the count himself had bestowed upon me before I had departed the first time. I greatly looked forward to seeing him again, being in his unique presence, learning from him.

"Upon our arrival in the vicinity of Castle Dracula, my heart nearly shattered. The great castle was empty, the grand palace in ruins! I did not know what had happened. I tracked down the band of gypsies who had worked in the service of the count. They remembered me and related the tale of what had become of Dracula. He had left his home and journeyed to London. Something had happened in London and he had tried to return to his homeland. Some of the citizens of London had followed him to his home mountains…and there, only a short distance from his great castle, they had ambushed and slain him! I had thought him the immortal sort, but he was gone!

"My mind and my soul filled with a rage and a fury unlike any I had ever known before…and I vowed to go to England, to London, and bring my own brand of Hell to the greatest city of the Western world! London would bow to me…and in the name of Dracula, I would destroy it!"

Watson's mind reeled with horror as he realized just how far the once proud, intelligent and confident Irene Adler had fallen into an abyss of dreadful insanity. He knew of no words that could describe his feelings toward the lunacy, the madness which he was now a witness to.

Chapter IX:
Season's End

"Destroy London?" Watson asked, startled by the absurdity of Adler's statement. "You must be joking. All you've done is drive several men insane. You're a minor murderess, yes, but the utter destruction of a great capitol city is far beyond even your abilities, Miss Adler!"

Irene Adler laughed. It was not the laughter of a sane woman.

"Dr. Watson, you underestimate me, as so many of your gender have done before you. The entire affair of which you speak was a simple experiment. I set up the Navigators of the Inner Planes and the group's seemingly clandestine gatherings as a means of testing the effects of my powder upon the human mind. The fates of those men; Bird, Cromwell, Morse, Hendricks and Cooper are evidence of its effectiveness. Now the entire city will feel the power of that miraculous substance. You see, Doctor, my underlings have stashed a large quantity of the dust in an important structure in the heart of London. Attached to the container which holds the powder is a powerful explosive device. When triggered, the resulting explosion will catapult the powder into the air, showering the city streets with the magical dust, causing madness, and eventual death by murder or suicide, on an epidemic scale. London will fall...and Dracula shall be avenged!"

Watson shook his head as rage grew in his heart.

"You truly are mad! I thank God that Holmes is not present to see you in the throes of this insanity!"

Adler turned away from Watson for a moment. She called out into the hallway.

"Percival, Gregor, the time has come. Go into the city, go to the clock, and do what must be done!"

Percival's reply could be heard through the curtains.

"Yes, Mistress, it shall be done!"

Watson could hear two sets of footsteps going down the stairs.

"You see, Dr. Watson, they are loyal enough to die for me, for the explosion will claim their lives, but I shall have my revenge! From the tower of Big Ben, the dust of Hell will rain down upon London!"

Watson jumped up from his seat. Instinctively, he reached into his coat for his revolver, but it was not there. That momentary lapse of memory cost him the advantage, and Adler took it from him. She grabbed a candlestick and struck a blow to his head. It was not enough to render him unconscious again, but he fell to his knees, hands flying up to his throbbing temple. Adler ran past him into the hallway.

On the ground floor of Kellington Manor, John Seward and Clarice Bird were preparing to make their way up the stairs to try to locate Watson. They heard sudden, pounding footsteps coming down the staircase. Unsure of who might be approaching, they ducked into a small closet to conceal themselves.

Percival and Gregor came down the stairs. Seward stepped out into the light and yelled for them to stop.

"Halt!" he said as he pointed his revolver in their direction. Gregor spun around, producing his large, curved knife as he turned. Seward did not hesitate. He shot the big gypsy in the chest. The room nearly shook as the immense corpse fell to the floor. Percival turned and tried to flee. Seward shot him in the back. Clarice screamed once and embraced Seward. As the two stared at the bodies of those who had just been shot, a third person came rapidly running down the same stairs. Irene Adler glared at Seward and Clarice.

"You've killed them!" she cried out. Seward took aim at her, but hesitated this time, unable to gun down a woman without consideration. Adler took advantage of his pause. She pressed her body against the wall and tapped on the wooden panel at her right hand. Seward and Clarice were shocked as the wall suddenly opened and then closed just as quickly, swallowing Irene Adler up in a concealed exit! Seward ran to the wall and pounded, but the mechanism had locked, leaving him to knock fruitlessly.

As he pounded in vain, Watson came hurrying down the stairs. A trickle of blood ran from his battered head, but the wound had not been serious enough to slow him.

"Seward, where is she? Where is the woman?" Watson shouted, not able to bring himself to speak Irene Adler's name aloud again.

Clarice was the first to reply.

"She went into the wall! She's gone!"

Watson waved his arm in the direction of the manor's front door.

"Get outside, quickly! We can't let her get away!"

The three ran outside as rapidly as possible, but the sight that greeted them made their hearts heavy with dread. Irene Adler's secret passageway had taken her to somewhere where a horse had been kept. It was a large, black steed, and it was now carrying her away from Kellington Manor at a fast pace.

"Where is she going, Watson?" asked Seward.

"To London, to Big Ben," Watson answered. "She's on a suicide mission to blast that infernal powder all over the city! We have to catch her!"

The trio ran the half-mile to where Watson and Seward had left the horses that had carried them to the manor. It was now dark but, luckily, the moon was full and bright, perhaps enough to provide sufficient light for them to ride.

Seward turned to Clarice.

"I'm sorry, I truly am, but we can't weigh down the horses with extra riders. You'll have to remain here. I swear I'll return for you as soon as I can."

He kissed her once on the cheek and mounted his horse. He took out Watson's revolver and handed it to him. Both men were now armed, but Seward reminded himself that he had just one bullet left in his own gun, while Watson's revolver held three.

The two doctors, both injured and weary, rode off into the night to try to save the lives and the sanity of the entire citizenry of London.

After an hour of the most rapid riding possible, Watson and Seward arrived outside the great, towering clock tower that the people of England had taken to calling Big Ben. It was midnight and the city streets were mostly deserted. They dismounted a few blocks away from the tower and ran the rest of the way in an attempt to appear less suspicious to anyone who might happen to see them there.

"We must get into the tower as quickly as possible," said Watson as they ran. "That woman is most resourceful and we must assume that she is already within."

They stopped in their tracks as they saw that two armed, uniformed guards stood in front of the most obvious entrance to the clock tower.

"I'll try to distract the guards," said Seward. "Run past them; you'll know when!"

"How will you accomplish that?" Watson asked.

Seward smiled.

"I've made a good living trying to understand insanity. Now it's time to test my ability at imitating it!"

Watson stood aside as Seward stripped off his coat and shirt. The younger of the two doctors let out a loud, whooping, banshee-like howl and ran, bare-chested, waving his bloodied, bandaged forearm in the air, straight at the two startled guards. The guards stared at him as he ran past them...and then they began to chase him.

Watson took the opportunity and ran like mad, right to the doors of Big Ben. He pushed the doors open and went into the immense clock tower. Inside he found his way to the stairs. Looking up, he saw that the steps went up and up, seemingly to the heavens themselves. He drew his revolver and began to climb.

Outside, the guards had caught Seward and tackled him to the ground. They confiscated his gun and tried to restrain him. He did not resist.

"What do you think you're doing, you lunatic?" asked one of the guards.

Seward grinned and answered the question.

"I'm saving your lives."

An eternity seemed to go by as Watson raced up the endlessly ascending flight of steps. His legs grew heavy, almost leaden. He felt more grateful than ever that he had kept himself in reasonably good condition for a man of his age. Upwards he climbed until his breath was labored and strained. Finally, he reached the top. Only a door stood between him and the room that sat behind the face of the great clock. He did not stop to think. He kicked the door open and exhaustedly stumbled inside.

He looked ahead. The room was dimly lit but he could make out the interior mechanism of the clock's huge face. Attached to the back of the clock-face was a large cloth sack which he assumed must have been full of the deadly, insanity-causing powder from the Orient. By the sack stood Irene Adler, her right hand perched upon a small wooden box from which dangled a fuse.

"Stop this madness, you foolish woman!" Watson barked.

Irene Adler laughed maniacally.

"You're too late, Watson."

She took her left hand from her coat pocket. Between her fingers was a match. She struck it and the flame ignited. She began to move the burning stick closer to the fuse.

Watson raised his gun.

"Do not make me do this!" he shouted desperately. In his mind, he could see Holmes. He could recall how the great detective had spoken as fondly and reverently of this woman as he had ever spoken of anyone. He knew that it would break the heart, or whatever sat where most men have hearts, of Sherlock Holmes to see her reduced to this madness. Still, he knew he had to act. He pushed all emotion and all hesitation aside and he pulled the trigger of his revolver.

The shot rang out. Irene Adler screamed. The bullet missed!

There was no blood, no impact sound of lead striking flesh. There was only a soft thump of the bullet hitting the tightly packed cloth bag, and the coughing sound as the powder flew from the torn bag and hit the woman in the face. She turned to Watson, her face an obscene mask of lunacy, the white dust outlining her features like the grotesque makeup of an unintentionally frightening clown.

She began to giggle. The laughter grew louder and louder. The match had burned down to the end of the stick and she dropped it as her fingertips felt the sudden heat. It extinguished upon the floor of the clock tower's chamber. She fell to her knees. Her eyes rolled back into her head and she collapsed into unconsciousness. Her last waking word was "Dracula."

Watson stood and waited until the dust settled to the floor. The bullet had only torn a small hole in the sack and most of the powder was still safely contained. He walked over to where Irene Adler lay. He took out his handkerchief and wiped the powder from her face. Then he lifted her limp body and began the exhausting task of carrying her down the many stairs. His primary emotion was great relief, accompanied by a hint of terrible sadness.

The next morning, after a few hours of much needed sleep, Watson, dressed in clean clothes, sat in the office of one of the British government's most trusted servants, a man whose name and duties were a carefully kept secret. The man's name was Mycroft Holmes.

Watson related the entire tale to the older brother of Sherlock Holmes. Mycroft nodded in response to the story's fantastic details.

"You've done a good thing, Watson. My younger brother would be suitably impressed, I think. You will, of course, keep the matter quiet, as will your friend Seward, I am sure."

Watson agreed that silence was the best possible course of action. To know that London had so nearly met with disaster would not sit well with the city's general population.

"I will mop up the messy details of the matter," Mycroft assured Watson. "Your part of the whole affair is over now. You have my gratitude…and that of Her Majesty as well."

Watson shook the hand of Mycroft Holmes and left the office, eager to hurry home to Baker Street for a cup of Mrs. Hudson's tea.

One day later, Watson and Seward stood on the London docks and watched as the *HMS Victorious* sailed out to sea. Of all those present on the docks or on the ship, only Watson, Seward, Mycroft Holmes and the ship's captain knew that *Victorious* carried a very strange cargo, a cloth sack filled with a powder that had very nearly been London's undoing. The sack would be, without ceremony or advertisement, dumped into the depths of the ocean, never again to be seen by human eyes, or touched by human hands. As the ship sailed out of view and vanished on the horizon, the two courageous doctors breathed a simultaneous sigh of relief.

Epilogue:
From the
Reminiscences of John H.
Watson, M.D.

One week after the sailing of *HMS Victorious*, I saw my friend John Seward again. The circumstances were happier ones this time as we shared a cab on our way to the Bird residence for a party in celebration of the eighteenth birthday of Miss Clarice Bird. It was a good evening.

One week after that, Seward and I received permission from the government to return to Kellington Manor one last time before the structure was demolished and the land upon which it had stood auctioned off. In one of the manor's bedchambers, we discovered the remains of the small fortune that had been given to Irene Adler by the mysterious Count Dracula (at the mention of who's name Seward turned, inexplicably, quite pale!). It was decided by the authorities that the money should be divided between the surviving victims of the terrible powder; Jacob Morse and Clarice Bird.

For Jacob Morse, who eventually fully regained his mental balance, the money provided the means by which he left London and his soiled reputation behind. No formal charges were ever filed against him and he left England to seek a new future in America.

For the Birds, the money was, perhaps, some small consolation for the loss of a devoted husband and father, Mr. Alexander Bird.

One year after the demolition of that awful mansion, it was my honor and privilege to be invited to attend a most joyous event, the wedding of Miss Clarice Bird. Her father being deceased, I was asked to escort her down the aisle, into the waiting embrace of her husband to be, Dr. John Seward.

Irene Adler never recovered from the effects of the powder she had sought to use against the innocent people of London. Seward arranged for her to be placed in an asylum far from the city. She died in that place a short time later. I never learned the exact details of her demise.

I never told Sherlock Holmes what had become of Miss Adler. I could not bear to. He did not hear of it from Mycroft either. Of that I am certain. On the occasions when she would happen to come up in conversation between Holmes and me, over the many years we had as friends, he continued to refer to her as he always had, simply as "The Woman."

HOUND-DOG HARKER

"Attack
of the
Electric Shark"

Chapter I:
The Hound Dog

For most of the many mostly happy years of their lives together, Mr. and Mrs. Jonathan Harker very rarely spoke to each other of the Incident. Their closest friends too, those who had experienced that dreadful chain of events along with the Harkers also rarely, if ever, spoke of those times. Dr. John Seward, Arthur Holmwood (known as Lord Godalming), and even the eccentric old professor, Abraham Van Helsing, knew better than to broach the subject lightly or frequently. Above all else, the Harkers and their circle of trusted confidantes all lived by an unspoken agreement to never, ever mention the Incident in the presence of the Harkers' son.

The child had been born not very long after the Incident. He was a strong, healthy boy from the start. He was christened with a long series of names, all of them in honor of those who had struggled together through those dark times. So, the boy was named Jonathan Arthur Abraham Quincy Harker. The name "John" would have been thrown in there as well, but Seward had the sense to argue that it would just be a needless repetition of the first syllable of "Jonathan," and politely declined the tribute.

As the boy grew into early childhood, his fearless curiosity and rugged energy began to remind his mother, Mina, of the attitude of their American friend, Quincy Morris, the one member of their small group who had not survived the Incident, sacrificing his own life in a brave manner so that the others might live. It was Mina who began to habitually call her son by his fourth name and the idea quickly caught on among the others, so that it was not long before the boy would not answer to any summons other than "Quincy."

Quincy Harker's childhood, during the very end of the 19th century and beginning years of the 20th, was a mostly happy one. His parents, while not excessively wealthy, were quite comfortable financially and their son received a first-rate education, going to private school and succeeding at his studies. He was an, intelligent, outgoing boy, one who made friends easily and made his parents proud. In his studies, he enjoyed history and had a natural tendency of curiosity about the sciences. He enjoyed athletics and was not afraid of physically rough activities, worrying his mother with his tendency to come home with bruises and scrapes, but always managing to avoid any more serious injuries.

It was at some point during his early adolescence that young Quincy grew quite certain that, at some point in the past, perhaps before he had been born, something very unusual had happened in the lives of his parents. He had no idea of the specific details of whatever the Incident might have been, and he always hesitated to question them on the matter, but he knew something. He was an observant boy and was quick to notice several seemingly minor, but conspicuous habits in his parents. Every evening, just as dusk approached, his mother would make her rounds of their home, scurrying from room to room and assuring her that every door was tightly locked, every window latched, no matter the weather outside. He also noted that an unusually large supply of garlic was perpetually kept in the family's pantry, though the pungent ingredient was very rarely used in Mina's cooking. Quincy's father, too, had his peculiarities. For one, Quincy had always observed a certain hesitation in Jonathan Harker whenever there was any reason to venture outdoors after dark. This struck the boy as being odd since, in all other respects, his father seemed to be a stalwart and respectable man. What could have occurred in the mysterious past to make the man so skittish at times?

Not knowing the exact nature of the Incident made Quincy more curious and fascinated than any certain knowledge would have and he became quite a follower of ghost stories and traditional superstitions. Even at a young age, the otherwise normal and bright child managed to learn more about grim and frightening folklore than most adults. Once, when his parents had both left the house for several hours, Quincy even searched his father's study and his mother's closet, hoping to find some sort of journal or diary that might contain some clue about the past of the Harkers, but he could find nothing. It was on this occasion that he discovered something else which he found unusual. Like many men, Jonathan Harker kept a revolver in his home, presumably to protect his family in the event of burglary. Young Quincy found his father's revolver while going through the study's desk drawers. The youth was quite surprised and puzzled to find that the gun was loaded with bullets of silver! Always, he wondered.

Young Mister Harker was a university student when the Great War began. He postponed the end of his studies and chose to enlist to serve his country. He did not hesitate to do so. Although he had not graduated from the university, there was a need for those worthy of serving as officers and Harker was deemed to be one of those capable individuals. He was commissioned at the rank of Lieutenant and was soon leading his men into combat against the forces of Germany.

It was one particular event that earned Lt. Quincy Harker his unique nickname. His unit had discovered a spy amongst themselves. A German sergeant had been masquerading as a British corporal, secretly gathering information to help his own nation's cause. By the time the traitor was discovered, he had fled the barracks. It was quite easy for the British troops to find the signs of his trail and determine which direction he had run off in. A chase began, though they were not sure how much time had elapsed since the spy had stolen away in the night. As the enlisted men began to grow tired from the pursuit, Lieutenant Harker proved to be unstoppable. Gathering tremendous reserves of energy from within himself, he endured, keeping up the chase long after his soldiers had passed the point of exhaustion. He was the last man to keep chasing, and the one who finally caught up to the spy and beat him senseless. So impressive was Harker's accomplishment that the oldest, most experienced of his non-commissioned officers, Sergeant Billy Baxter, blurted out the words, "That Harker's like a hound from Hell, he is; a hound dog from Hell!" The nickname stuck and the young lieutenant was henceforth known among his men as Hound Dog Harker.

During the course of the war, Hound Dog Harker proved to be a brave soldier and capable commanding officer, decorated many times and eventually being promoted to Captain.

After the war ended, Harker was asked by the British government to go into the intelligence services, which he did. He quickly gained a reputation as a man who could be called on to fulfill the role of spy, detective, saboteur, or troubleshooter whenever needed. He was often assigned to cases that had an apparently supernatural nature to them, mostly because of his reputation as a man who had acquired extensive knowledge of such an odd subject. It was not the sort of thing that many Army officers knew much about.

A decade passed and Captain Quincy "Hound Dog" Harker continued to serve the British Empire in the way that only he could. He was considered one of the most unique resources at the disposal of Her Majesty's government. He was paid quite handsomely for his services and was able to afford a large, spacious, and expensive apartment in London.

By the time he was in his early thirties, he was living a life of semi-luxury combined with thrilling adventure. He was a happy man, despite the dangers of his profession.

It was not alone that Harker carried out many of his assignments for the government. When he had returned to England after the conclusion of the war, he took with him two men, his two confidantes and loyal friends. The first was Sergeant Billy Baxter, a decade older than Harker, but always willing to follow his captain's orders. The other had been the company clerk under Harker's command. His name was Calvin "Picky" Pickover. He had been a corporal in Harker's unit, but had come from a long line of professional butlers. For generation, his family had served some of England's richest families. Although Harker was not wealthy to that degree, he had earned the loyalty of Pickover during the great conflict and so Picky had chosen to stick with his captain, acting just as his father and his father's father had acted towards their own employers.

Baxter and Pickover were equally loyal to Quincy Harker, but were opposites in many other ways. Sergeant Baxter was not a smart man, occasionally dim-witted and extremely stubborn, but he was very, very brave, always willing to charge headfirst into a dangerous situation, often without thoroughly thinking it through. If Harker was a hound dog, Baxter was pure pit bull. Picky Pickover, on the other hand, was quite intelligent and usually had a novel idea in a difficult situation, but he was typically soft-spoken and would flinch and cringe in the face of danger. Despite their individual idiosyncrasies, both men were good friends and loyal companions to Captain Harker.

Chapter II:
The Frenchman

Pierre Goulet was a very wealthy man. He was in his mid-forties, a tall man, thin, with an exceptionally long nose and a thin moustache that quivered and waved from both sides of his long face as he walked or moved his head. His father had been a successful French businessman and the son had inherited the father's riches. When the senior Goulet had died, it had been under suspicious circumstances and the son was a suspect, but no proof of wrongdoing was ever found, and so no formal charges were ever presented against Pierre Goulet. So, the son took the father's fortune and did with it as he pleased.

From a very young age, Pierre Goulet, who possessed great intelligence, had been fascinated by maps and globes. It was not ordinary maps that held him in rapt attention, but strange ones, old ones, somewhat primitive and curious maps. The sort of maps and globes that depicted, in the spaces between land masses, in the oceans that cover two-thirds of the world, monsters and great serpents of the sea. At some point in Goulet's youth, he had seen some of those dramatically depicted sea beasts on a map or a globe, and the images had gained a permanent foothold in his imagination, becoming something of a personal archetype to him.

When he grew up, he engaged in an intense study of geography, cartography, and learned more than most about the layout of the world, the shapes of the seas, and exactly what those mysterious old maps had been trying to portray in their primitive ways. To a great extent, those maps and their fantastic scenes of serpentine monsters became an obsession to Pierre Goulet.

It was on one particular night, in the late, late hours, as he sat in the library of his large home on the French coast, that Pierre Goulet had a sudden, life-altering revelation. He had been smoking his pipe, absent-mindedly staring at a replica of an antique globe, and trying to overcome a bout of insomnia, when his mind went spinning towards a certain wild theory and his point of view of history and the world in which he lived changed dramatically.

"Sacre bleu," he shouted loudly as he jumped up from his chair, "I have been so blind! Perhaps there is more here than I dared to dream!"

His pipe fell to the floor, forgotten in his sudden jolt of inspiration. He picked up the globe from the desk, held it up in front of his face and stared at it with wonder and the lust for power glowing in his eyes.

In that one moment of insight and inspiration, two trains of thought had collided in Goulet's mind and imagination. On one hand, he had always known that the antique maps he had long studied were not quite exact in how they depicted the shape of the continents and oceans, having been drawn in a time when cartography was less exact than it had become in the twentieth century. By mathematically analyzing these maps, Goulet had been able to approximate what parts of the world were actually represented upon them. He had written a key, a method by which he could translate the locations shown on those maps into the more exact geographical information that would prove to be of great use to a modern mariner. By this method, Goulet could combine the information upon various different maps and pinpoint a location that might be hinted at by the grotesque looking monsters shown on those old parchments.

Secondly, Goulet had always been fascinated by the idea, spoken of in whispers by those scientists, anthropologists and archeologists who feared ruining their scholarly reputations by being more vocal about their theories, that Earth had once been the home of much more advanced civilizations. The idea was not a new one and could be found to be hinted at in many an old, long out of print book; the idea that advanced technology had once been in common use among some of the peoples of the world, technology far more powerful than that of the 1930s!

On that night, unable to sleep and sitting in his study with his pipe lit, Pierre Goulet happened upon an amazing idea. What if, he thought, his mind spinning, those monsters on those maps were merely a corruption of something else, something far older? What if the later copiers of those maps had placed images of great serpents where there had once, on the earliest copies of those maps, been images of great, fearful oceangoing vessels, the ships of those whispered-of antediluvian dynasties and ancient civilizations?

Goulet's mood upon the sudden formation of that theory was almost more than he could stand. If it was correct, he knew, and he could find those ancient vessels, if there was anything left of them, he could grow rich to a degree far beyond anything his father had ever known. Then and there, Pierre Goulet vowed to devote his time, his energy, and his fortune to investigating this grand new idea that had taken form in his mind.

He spent much of the next five years further researching his theory. When he was certain that he was correct, when he could resist the temptation to travel to the sites on those maps no longer, he began to put together the things he would need to progress his plans to the next stage.

He purchased a small fleet of ships; small vessels, but fast and stealthy. He hired enough men to provide adequate crews for those ships. He had two requirements when selecting his oceangoing employees; they had to be seasoned sailing men, and they had to be willing to do whatever they were told, whether or not it overstepped the boundaries of the law. Basically, he had manned his ships with a small navy of mercenary mariners.

Goulet set his men and their ships to the task of sailing to each of the locations he had decided upon, one at a time, to look for anything unusual that might be present at each of the scenes.

Fortunately for Goulet's quest, the period of time in which he began his search was the period of time in which the equipment needed to search deep below the waves was becoming available. Goulet purchased diving suits and other underwater swimming apparatus, making certain that experienced divers were among those mercenary mariners that he hired to assist him in his search.

Goulet's examinations of the first two spots he had chosen had proven fruitless. He assumed that his lack of success might be due to one of two things: perhaps he had miscalculated the locations, or perhaps time and the ocean waves had either completely corroded what he had expected to find, or swept it to a different location. Never once did it occur to him that his precious theory might be wrong.

The third site would prove different. One of Goulet's ships, a yacht sized boat filled with all sorts of equipment had found the location that Goulet had chosen for that particular day's search. The ship sat in the Atlantic Ocean, in a place where the waters were deep enough to conceal a vessel of considerable size, but not so deep that such a ship would have sunken to a depth that man could not endure in proper diving gear.

Goulet's chief diving expert was a man called Angus McKay, a big, muscular Scotsman. He stood upon the deck in his thick, heavy diving suit as his assistant put the helmet, with its fishbowl-like window, upon his head and fastened it on.

"Here we go again, Captain!" was the last phrase to come from his mouth before he dove from the ship's deck into the Atlantic waters. Pierre Goulet nodded to himself and hoped that this time, on this third attempt, Angus McKay would resurface with news of some kind of success. He watched as his diver vanished beneath the water's surface.

Ten minutes later, McKay's helmeted head popped back up in sight of the ship's deck. He waved his hand frantically in the air, signaling for the men on deck to help him back on board by pulling in the line that tethered him to the vessel. Within minutes he was back aboard. Goulet paced the deck impatiently as McKay's helper unfastened the diving helmet from his boss. Finally, the heavy helmet was lifted off and McKay spoke excitedly.

"It's down there, Captain! It's big as a mountain and it's the weirdest, most beautiful thing I've ever seen in all my years!"

Goulet's heart jumped. He had been right! All his years of searching and spending his inherited fortune on his quest, the quest others thought was hopeless madness, had come to something.

"Get my diving suit!" Goulet barked at his men. "McKay, get ready to go down again. You must take me to it!"

Fifteen minutes later, another splash could be heard by the men on the ship's deck. It was louder this time, as there were now two men diving into the Atlantic. Under the water, Goulet followed McKay. Soon, it was visible. There, under the sea, hidden from the sight of any but those who knew where to look, was the hulking remains of the strangest, most alien-looking vessel that anyone in known human history had ever laid eyes upon.

Had the two men not been underwater, Pierre Goulet's gasp would have been audible. He swam up to the long-lost ship. It was enormous, much longer than his yacht-sized exploring vessel. The surface was metallic and sleek. Despite its great size, it looked fast and maneuverable. To Goulet, it was a breathtakingly beautiful thing to behold.

He treaded water just above the top of the ship, which had sunk upright and rested peacefully upon the ocean floor, not very deep at all, in water shallow enough to let adequate sunlight penetrate to the scene. There was only a small outer deck area, so Goulet made the assumption that it must have been fully submersible, a very old, and very advanced, very large submarine! He found what appeared to be a hatch atop the vessel. There seemed to be a small button on that hatch. Summoning his courage and resolve, Goulet reached out his hand, in its thick, clumsy diving glove, and pressed down on the button with his thumb.

As soon as the small button was pressed, the shocked Goulet thought the entire Earth had begun to shake violently. He panicked for a moment, and then realized that it was not the Earth moving, but the ship beneath him! He had activated something, a mechanism of some kind. The water bubbled and turned warm around him. Angus McKay swam over to join him and they clung to the top of the ship as it rose, quickly and forcefully, to the surface of the sea. As it broke the surface, the entire crew of Goulet's search vessel had run out onto the deck to witness what was happening. The great, ancient ship exploded from out of its resting place beneath the waves and roared to the surface, its discoverer and his chief diver standing triumphantly atop it! The sailors of Goulet's ship gasped in shock and awe as they looked at the huge, once-hidden vessel, its massive form humming with reawakened power, electricity, its long hull shaped by its long-forgotten makers to resemble the form of a gigantic and fearsomely terrible Great White Shark! McKay and Goulet helped each other remove their diving helmets. They stood atop the amazing thing they had just found and activated and grinned triumphantly.

"I was right! I have found it...and it is mine!" shouted Pierre Goulet, all his efforts rewarded in one dramatic scene that would change his life forever.

Chapter III:
When the Shark
Bites

Six weeks later, Pierre Goulet felt as if he were on top of the world. He had no need for his small fleet of ships now; he had his new prize, his great floating fortress which he had fished up from the depths of the sea and the depths of the past. He had transferred his entire entourage of mercenary mariners to this wondrous new vessel and set them all to the task of learning to operate what Goulet was convinced could be the greatest weapon that one man had ever possessed. He had named Angus McKay his first mate and things had begun to progress smoothly. They had named their amazing vessel *The Electric Shark*!

The *Shark* was massive, multi-decked and sleekly designed. It apparently ran on a powerful electrical current, although Goulet could not quite figure out how its batteries had remained charged through all those generations under the ocean waves. What had become of its crew also remained a mystery, as no trace of any bodies or skeletons or even scraps of clothing had been found aboard. The ship was now manned with about fifty sailors, hand-picked by Goulet and McKay. They had learned to operate the *Shark* quite proficiently in a short time; the apparently ancient technology with which the vessel was equipped seemed to respond swiftly to any manipulation of its controls. It could submerge or surface quickly, travel at great speeds both above and below the water's surface, and had several very large gun-like weapons, though Goulet had not yet found the proper place or circumstances in which to test the ship's destructive potential.

His incredible new seafaring home now at his command, Goulet sat in his shipboard cabin and lit his pipe, thinking back to the night when his insomnia had led him to come up with his wild theory, the theory that had brought him to where he now sat. He pondered how to best use the ship to his own benefit. What would he do next?

From his window in Kingston, Jamaica, Roger Mason looked out upon the Caribbean Sea. He sat back in his desk chair and lit a cigarette. Mason was the president of the British Bank's Kingston branch, the largest money-lending and savings facility in the island's capitol. He loved Jamaica and enjoyed his work. He was well paid and enjoyed the magnificent and usually agreeable warm, clear weather that his island was blessed with. Mason was in his late forties and had lived in Jamaica for nearly two decades, having been appointed to a clerk's position in the bank after ending a term of service as a lieutenant in the British navy. He found that he was good at what he did and quickly earned a series of promotions, rapidly advancing to the position of bank president. A hefty man, not athletic but not slovenly and fat either, Mason was the type of man who radiated an aura of calm confidence most of the time, earning him the respect, if not adoration, of his employees. A single man with no relatives, his only real vice was his occasional, and as secretive as possible, perusal of the island's prostitutes. Mason's office was on the second floor of the bank building; he often went there for an hour or two in the late morning after inspecting the status of the bank's operations. He would sit down, smoke, and get lost in thought as he looked out upon the calm surrounding seas. On this particular morning, his silent reverie was suddenly interrupted by a knock upon the office door.

"Enter," Mason said in response to the knock. He was used to having one of his employees come to the door needing assistance with one problem or another, so he thought nothing of the knock now. The door opened and a man whom Mason did not recognize entered. He was an early middle-aged man, tall and thin with a moustache. He smiled as he walked into Mason's office.

"Can I help you, Sir?" Mason asked without rising from his chair.

"Yes, Monsieur," answered Pierre Goulet happily. "I am here to rob your bank, and you are going to assist me without argument."

Mason leapt up from his seat in one swift motion.

"Are you insane?" he snapped at the Frenchman. "I don't see a gun in your hand. I need only shout out for the guards and I'll see you hauled from here in irons! But...I am going to assume that this is some sort of joke that one of my workers has enlisted you to play on me. You have the chance to turn around and leave this office now."

Goulet laughed in his sly, nasal tone.

"Monsieur Mason, I assure you that this is no joke. I am here to show you something that will very easily convince you that I am serious."

He reached into his jacket pocket and produced a pair of binoculars. He walked over to where Roger Mason stood. He handed the binoculars to Mason.

"Take these glasses," said Goulet. "I want you to look out of that very large window you have here. Look out over the beautiful sea. Out there, among those peaceful tides, perhaps a mile from the shores of this island, you will see an ordinary ocean buoy floating and bobbing along. Do you see it?"

Mason, still looking through the binoculars, grunted to affirm that he saw the buoy.

"Good," Goulet continued. "Now I want you to look past the buoy, perhaps a thousand feet past it. You do not see anything, do you? You see only the water; the bright, blue water. Be patient, Monsieur Mason. In a moment, you will see something quite extraordinary."

Mason looked just a bit farther out to sea through his binoculars. The previously calm seas beyond the buoy had begun to show signs of movement. At first it was just a slight disturbance of the water's surface, then a more active churning of the waves, then a great and sudden splashing of massive amounts of waters being thrown upwards with great force, as if some great leviathan were erupting forcefully from beneath the waves. Mason gasped in astonishment as the *Electric Shark* came bursting into his line of sight.

"My God!" he exclaimed. "What in the name of the devil is it?"

"That, my dear Monsieur Mason, is my small toy," answered Goulet. "I present to you…*The Electric Shark*! Now I ask you to watch and be amazed by what is about to happen next!"

Mason kept his eyes locked on the scene that unfolded through the lenses of the binoculars. The immense and ancient vessel that Goulet had announced had now fully surfaced and sat upon the sea. The wooden buoy still bobbed in its place just a bit closer to the shore. As Mason observed, a small hatch opened atop the ship. Something rose up from the opening, a piece of machinery that looked like a gun of some sort. Without warning or prelude, a blast of energy, of electrical force, shot out from the cannon and instantly demolished the buoy! Splintering wood flew and plumes of smoke rose! It was a scene of utter floating destruction. Mason gasped.

"My God! What in the name of the devil is it?"

"My God!" the bank president muttered. He took the binoculars from his eyes and turned to Pierre Goulet, shock written in his expression.

"How have you acquired such a thing? Where...?"

Goulet laughed almost maniacally.

"Monsieur Mason...the range of that weapon is most impressive. I could easily instruct my men to aim it at this very bank, or at the main marketplace of Kingston, or at one of your local schools! They have been given very exact instructions to fire upon those very targets should I not return or contact them within a very specific window of time. You are going to hand over to me a very large sum of money...or I shall rain hellfire down upon you and the citizens of this island! Is that understood?"

Roger Mason nodded. He was no coward, but he was not a foolish man either. He had been awed and frightened by the destructive display he had just witnessed, and he had no desire to see innocents hurt. He summoned two of his most trusted employees and had them gather up a large sum of cash. This money was placed in two bulky bags; large, but not too heavy for one man to carry, and given to Pierre Goulet, who whistled mischievously as he walked along the sunny streets of Kingston, Jamaica and back to the small rowboat that was waiting to carry him back to his much more imposing warship.

When the Frenchman had gone, Roger Mason did what he knew he had to do; he contacted the British government and gave a full report of the extraordinary events of that afternoon.

Chapter IV:
Taking Flight

"You're bluffing, Captain. You can't fool this old soldier!" shouted Billy Baxter as he waved his hand of cards at Quincy Harker. The poker game had been going on for over an hour. Baxter and Harker had gone through half a bottle of Scotch and the ashtray was overflowing with Harker's cigarette butts and the remains of Baxter's big cigars. Harker laughed at Baxter's accusation and was about to reveal his hand when Calvin Pickover, his loyal butler, burst into the room.

"What is it, Picky?" asked Harker, a bit annoyed at the interruption of a very intense game.

"Begging your pardon, Captain Harker," said the butler, "But Colonel Sharpe is on the telephone and he wishes to speak with you. Judging by his tone of voice, it is a matter of urgency."

Harker dropped the cards on the table. He no longer cared whether Baxter saw his hand. The game was irrelevant in Harker's mind at that moment. A call from Colonel Sharpe could mean only one thing; Captain Quincy "Hound Dog" Harker's services were required by the British Government, and that meant that Harker's recent span of boredom and inactivity was over. It probably also meant that some sort of intrigue and danger would confront Harker in the very near future, and he welcomed such things.

He walked out of the room where the poker game had been taking place, leaving the old sergeant, Baxter, sitting there puffing on his stogie. Harker, a six foot tall, dark haired, strongly built man, calmly went into his in-residence office and gestured for his butler, Pickover, to leave the room and close the door behind him. Harker picked up the telephone.

"Yes, Colonel," Harker said in his military voice, the voice that came back to him instinctively and automatically whenever he had reason to talk to his superior in the Intelligence Service.

"Captain Harker," replied the voice of Colonel Thurman Sharpe, "I realize that it's late, but I need to see you at once. I expect you in my office in an hour, and pack a case. You'll be leaving London for a few days."

"Can I bring Baxter and Picky?" asked Harker.

The Colonel snorted on the other end of the line. He could never quite understand why Harker insisted on bringing his old sergeant and his butler on all his assignments, but he was willing to put up with the captain's little eccentricities if it meant that the job at hand would get done.

"If you must," said Colonel Sharpe, and Harker heard the abrupt sound of the phone hanging up.

Harker opened the office door and shouted joyfully into the next room.

"Picky, pack the bags! We're taking a little trip!"

A short time later, Quincy Harker walked into the office of Colonel Sharpe. Baxter and Pickover had waited outside, neither one of them having the official security clearance to be in on the briefing, although Harker would fill them in on the details as soon as he saw them again, and he knew that the colonel would not object.

Thurman Sharpe looked up from behind his desk and scowled at Harker. The scowl did not mean that Sharpe was angry at Harker; it was simply the colonel's standard facial expression. He was a big man, the type who had always reminded Harker of a walrus, though it was not obesity, but thick muscle and solid stature that caused such an appearance. Though the colonel was not a young man by any means, he had the look of a man who could still hold his own in a physical struggle.

"Sit down, Captain Harker," the colonel muttered, preferring not to waste time with polite greetings. Harker sat across from Sharpe's desk and his commanding officer began to relate the reasons he had been summoned at that late hour.

"There was an incident in Jamaica several hours ago; in Kingston, to be more precise. It was bank robbery; by no means a typical stick-up, either. It seems that some fellow just waltzed into the bank president's office and handed him a pair of spy glasses. The president, a man called Mason, looked out over the sea and witnessed some kind of a ship, a submersible apparently, rise up out of the water and blast a buoy to smithereens with some kind of cannon, electrically powered cannon! Mason's visitor told him that the range of that gun was enough to reach right into the heart of Kingston. Mason believed him and handed over a large sum of cash. I didn't see this display with my own eyes, so I can't say whether Mason did the right thing or not, but that's what happened."

Harker nodded, indicating that he had understood everything that Colonel Sharpe had said.

"What do we know about this 'visitor,' as you called him?" was Harker's first question.

The colonel lit his pipe and answered.

"According to Mason's report of the incident, the man was French, early middle-aged, didn't give his name. That's about all we know so far. He called his ship...*The Electric Shark*! An overly flamboyant name if you ask me, but that's what Mason said it looked like; a gigantic steel shark, rising up from the water and raining fire on that buoy."

"So what do I do?" Harker requested more information.

The colonel laughed, not pleasantly, but with a tone of impatience behind it.

"What do you think you do, Harker? You'll be on the next possible flight to Kingston, along with that thick-headed old sergeant and that whiny butler of yours! Now get going! Find out all you can about the situation. This is the sort of weird business you seem to have a knack for. I don't know why that is, but that's how things are."

Harker had no intention of sticking around any longer. He could tell that the colonel had no patience for further questions. He left the office and raced to the car.

"Get us to Croydon Airport, Picky; double time!"

The flight to Jamaica was uneventful. Harker and Baxter were able to finish their poker game. Picky Pickover, who had a phobia when it came to flying, nervously stared out the window for most of the trip, his teeth always just on the borderline of beginning to chatter. It was a bright, sunny, quite balmy afternoon in Kingston when the trio disembarked. Harker sent his two loyal traveling companions, with their bags, to their hotel while he immediately made his way to the Kingston offices of the British Bank. Dressed in a light tan suit with white shoes and a fedora to match the suit, Quincy Harker blended in well with those people, both residents of the islands and visitors from various nations, who went about their business and pleasures on the bustling Kingston streets. He reached the bank, was greeted by the head clerk, flashed his identification card, and was quickly escorted up a short flight of stairs to the office of the bank's branch president, Roger Mason.

"Captain Harker, I was told to expect you," said Mason as he extended his hand in greeting. "I can't tell you how hopeful I am that you might be able to get to the bottom of this rotten business. I'm quite ashamed of myself for letting that scoundrel make off with such a sum of money... but I could truly see no alternative. He stooped so low as to threaten the innocent citizens of Kingston...even the children!"

Harker nodded and Mason continued on without pause.

"I don't know if I can be of much more help to you, though, Captain. Everything I know was in my report to your superiors. I provided them with a description of the man, a description of his strange ship, monstrous thing that it was, and I told them that he was French. Other than that, I haven't the slightest clue about the matter!"

That was all that Harker was able to get from Roger Mason. The bank president was clearly shaken to the core by the weird robbery, but Harker knew he really had already reported all the information he had. Harker left the bank and puffed on a cigarette as he made his way to the hotel to rejoin Billy Baxter and Picky Pickover.

Harker arrived at the hotel and went directly up to his room. It was in the middle of three adjoining rooms, with the quarters of his two friends on either side. Tired from the flight and frustrated by not quite knowing how to proceed in his investigation, he tossed aside his hat and flopped down on the room's large, luxurious bed. He had just started to relax his body and let his sharp mind begin to work on the problem when a rapid knocking began on the door to his left. He stood up, walked over, and opened it.

"Captain Harker, you're back! Thank goodness! Just after Mr. Baxter and I arrived, there was an urgent telephone call for you, sir!" said a frantic Picky Pickover as the door opened.

"Well who was it?" begged Harker for an answer. "Calm down, Picky! Don't forget to breathe!"

"It was Colonel Sharpe, sir!" answered the usually nervous manservant. "I'm afraid he wouldn't tell me what it was about; he insisted that you call him in London immediately upon your return here!"

Knowing that such an urgent message would be unwise to ignore, Harker rather brusquely shut the door in Pickover's face, retrieved his hat from where he had dropped it, left his room, and raced down to the hotel lobby. He entered one of the five telephone booths along the lobby's wall and shut the door behind him. He connected to the operator in London and spoke a certain seven-digit number, a code that would put him in direct contact with the private line in Colonel Thurman Sharpe's office. He heard the phone ring three times and Sharpe's gruff voice came over the line.

"It's about time you called back, Harker. There's been a lucky development and I need you to get ready for another trip; not as far this time, but at a quicker pace!"

Harker was relieved and exhilarated. He had been worried that his questioning of Roger Mason had been a dead end. If some new development had occurred, perhaps the case was back on the right track.

"What's happened, Colonel?" asked the "Hound Dog" with anticipation. Colonel Sharpe began to explain.

"You see, Captain, this strange vessel of the Frenchman's surfaced off the coast of a small, unnamed island about a hundred miles from Kingston. A British plane happened to be in the area and the pilots got a fairly decent look at the thing. It's as big as Roger Mason said it was, and just as unusual. They were in flight and couldn't exactly stop for a better look or, unfortunately, take any photographs of it, but at least we've now got some idea of its recent whereabouts."

"There's a British Naval vessel heading to Kingston at full speed as I speak to you. It's the Admiral-class battle cruiser, *HMS Hood*. Her captain is David Fuller, an old friend of mine. You're to meet the ship at Kingston's docks as soon as she arrives, which should be within the hour. Captain Fuller will take you along to go out looking for that Electric Shark, or whatever the Frenchman called it. If you find it, the orders are to engage it only if you and Fuller agree that you have a fair chance against it. Do not do anything foolish, Harker. Is that understood?"

Harker hesitated for a moment. He wondered just how the colonel defined the boundaries between "foolish" and "heroic."

"Yes, Sir, it's understood," he finally answered. "I'll be on my way to meet the *Hood* and its captain right away."

Colonel Sharpe, ever direct and blunt, said nothing else. Harker heard the line click. When the call was ended, he ran up the stairs and back to his room. He grabbed his suitcase and, without bothering to open the doors to the two adjoining rooms, shouted for his two companions to come to him.

"Baxter, Picky, I need you both in here now!"

Seconds later, the faithful butler and the grizzled veteran sergeant burst through the doors on either side of Harker.

"Listen, boys," said the young captain, "I'm to meet up with one of our fine Navy's battle cruisers in a little while. Baxter, you're coming along for the ride. Picky, sorry old man, but you're to remain here. I need you to stick around the hotel in case the colonel calls with any further instructions. Anyway, I know you tend to get a bit seasick! Baxter, let's get going!"

With that, Captain Quincy Harker and retired Sergeant Billy Baxter were out the door and off to the docks, not wanting to waste any more time sitting around a Kingston hotel room.

Chapter V:
The Boys on the Hood

The British fleet's largest battleship, *HMS Hood* was an impressive sight as it sailed into Kingston harbor. The ship was a massive vessel, weighing nearly fifty-thousand tons. It was 860 feet long and 104 feet across the beam. With a speed of thirty knots and a great number of guns and torpedo tubes, the *Hood* was a force to be reckoned with.

Quincy Harker smiled when he saw the ship and began to quicken his pace towards it. Billy Baxter, limping slightly from the ache of an old war wound that occasionally acted up, did his best to keep up with his captain. Once aboard, Harker was greeted warmly by the commanding officer, who extended his hand.

"Welcome aboard, Captain Harker. Colonel Sharpe speaks most highly of you. I'm David Fuller."

The ship's captain led Harker and Baxter up to the main command deck of the ship. There was no delay in getting underway. Fuller barked some orders to the engineers and helm and the great battle cruiser roared out of the Kingston docks at full speed. Harker took out a cigarette and lit it as he watched Jamaica move off into the distance. He offered one to Captain Fuller, but the naval officer declined.

While Harker was becoming acquainted with Captain Fuller, Billy Baxter wandered about the bridge, examining the controls and instruments as if he knew something about the operations of naval vessels, which he certainly did not. He began to poke and prod at a panel of switches and levers and had to be reprimanded, as politely as possible, by one of the petty officers. Baxter almost shot a snide comment back at the young sailor, but quickly bit his tongue, turned away, and pranced back over to where Harker and Fuller stood.

"A mighty fine ship you've got here, Skipper!" Baxter cheerfully announced to Fuller, trying to hide his embarrassment by being overly enthusiastic about the experience of being aboard the *Hood*. Harker, who was used to the old sergeant's behavior, kindly but firmly, indicated that he should stay out of the way.

"Keep a close watch on everyone, Sergeant, but try not to get in the way. We're guests here and can help this mission along by standing aside until we're needed."

Baxter, his desire to act outweighed by his respect for Quincy Harker, did as he was told. The ship sailed smoothly but rapidly away from the Jamaican island and the day grew into dusk and then night. Captain Fuller gave Harker and Baxter a full tour of the ship, at least the parts that non-naval personnel were allowed access to. After the tour, Harker and Baxter were invited to dine with the senior officers. A good time was had by all as Harker regaled them all with tales of action he had seen in the Great War. Despite the light and cheerful mood in the mess hall, not one of those present forgot for even a moment that they were sailing toward potentially grave danger and a possible fight against a ship with undetermined, but very frightening armament.

Dinner was followed by rest for Harker and Baxter as they settled into their temporary bunks and promptly fell asleep. They had both grown used to being able to get a good night's sleep even when danger was imminent. In the morning, both awoke at the first sign of dawn's light showing her face through the portholes. Harker jumped down from his bunk first, pulled on his shirt, trousers and shoes, then ordered Baxter to dress and follow him up to the bridge. Arriving at the ship's command deck, they were greeted by Captain Fuller, who reported their location, heading and speed. No sign of anything unusual had thus far been spotted by the ship's crew.

By noon, it had turned out to be a beautiful day at sea. The waters were calm and the skies were clear. Captain Fuller left his first lieutenant in charge on the bridge and went below to show Harker around the engine room. Billy Baxter had made fast friends with the sergeant major of the ship's complement of Royal Marines and had gone off with him, the two veterans trading war stories.

As Harker and Fuller conversed in the smoky, noisy bowels of the *Hood*, the General Quarters alarm suddenly began to blare!

"We have to get to the bridge!" shouted the ship's captain and began to rush to the ladders that connected the decks. Harker followed close behind. The two captains reached the ship's command center and the first lieutenant explained the reason for the alert.

"Captain, it's appeared, sir! It's massive! What are your orders?"

Fuller and Harker looked ahead through the bridge windows. The waves thrashed and churned. Gone was the calm sea, replaced by the whirling maelstrom brought on by the sudden surfacing of *The Electric Shark*!

"Helm, stand ready to move at my orders!" barked Fuller. "Torpedo men and gunners; get to your stations and at the ready!"

Behind the excited captain, Quincy Harker stood with his hands behind his back, his posture one of confidence and ease. It was not that he was not concerned about what might happen next, but he had long since learned to keep his mind calm and his thoughts lucid even in the most perilous situations.

"Captain Fuller," said Harker softly, "should you need me to do anything, say the word."

Ahead of the British battle cruiser, the gigantic and mysterious vessel loomed, causing fear and dread to rise up in the hearts and minds of the *Hood*'s officers and men. As if in answer to all their unspoken questions, a loud booming voice suddenly came across the air. The voice was tinged by the electrical crackle of the loudspeaker with which *The Electric Shark* was equipped.

"Crew of British warship…you are most likely very afraid…as well you should be at this time!" said the voice, which was firm and male, with a pronounced French accent. "You should also consider yourselves very fortunate, for you are now to witness the awesome power of the greatest vessel of war to sail the seas in many centuries! Gentlemen, officers, sailors, I present to you…*The Electric Shark!*"

Before the eyes of Fuller, Harker, and the terrified bridge crew of the British vessel, the tremendous ancient warship in front of them began to glow with a weird energy. They watched in horror as the hatches along the ship's roof began to open and strange guns appeared to rise up from their formerly concealed positions.

"Brace for impact!" shouted Captain Fuller as beams of light and electricity shot forth from the bizarre pirate vessel and the *Hood* was shaken and rocked as if it were besieged by a land bound tremor!

Sailors were thrown from their positions, men fell upon the deck floor, and Captain Fuller managed to stay standing by holding onto a handrail. Quincy Harker stumbled a bit but also managed to keep his footing.

"Return fire!" commanded Fuller. The *Hood*'s guns barked out the rat-tat-tat sound of ammunition being thrown full-force at the *Electric Shark*, but that noise was followed by the disappointing clank of the British shells rebounding harmlessly off the thick hull, composed of some heretofore unknown elemental steel, of the great enemy ship! The captain and men of the British battle cruiser stared in stunned silence, awaiting the next wave of attack, expecting the worst. No more violence came. The booming loudspeaker voice of the Frenchman came across the air again.

"You were told of what was to come, men of the British navy…and now you have seen and felt it for yourselves. I shall not sink you, shall not send you to graves beneath these waves, for I wish for you to perform a duty that is sacred to me! You shall go back to that miserable prison that you call 'civilization' and you shall tell all the men of your country and other powerful nations of what you have seen here today. From this day forward, I am the ruler of the seas! You may tell the world of me! My name is Pierre Goulet; Admiral Pierre Goulet. The oceans of the world belong to me; to me…and *The Electric Shark!*"

With that great burst of pompous speech, the mighty battleship from antediluvian times suddenly, unstoppably, sank beneath the waters of the Caribbean Sea. The *Electric Shark* had vanished from sight, but it would not soon vanish from the memories of the twelve-hundred men who manned *The Hood*, or their two guests, Captain Quincy Harker and retired Sergeant Billy Baxter.

"My God!" exclaimed Captain David Fuller, breaking the stunned silence on the bridge. "How in the name of all that is holy can we ever hope to combat such a foe?"

Quincy Harker, never humbled no matter what his brave eyes beheld, put a reassuring hand on the ship captain's shoulder and spoke two sentences.

"We will find a way, Captain. There will always be a way."

Within minutes, the bridge had received complete damage and casualty reports from every part of the ship. The damage was mostly minor, which led Harker to believe that Goulet had intended to put on a show, rather than do any real harm; he had been trying to impress more than injure. There had been some injuries to the crew, but none had died; the most serious injuries had been several concussions and a broken leg. The oddest thing reported was that one of the ship's small lifeboats had seemed to have disappeared. Captain Fuller voiced his assumption that the boat had probably been knocked into the sea in the wake of the enemy vessel's submerging, but an alternative answer occurred to Quincy Harker. Hoping he was wrong, but fearing he was correct, Harker excused himself from the captain's company and raced down the corridors and decks to his temporary quarters. He shoved open the door and went in. He let out a sigh of annoyance when he saw that a note had been quickly scrawled on a torn sheet of stationary and dropped upon his bunk.

"Captain," said the note, "I've gone to get on that big boat. Somebody's got to go and I figure I'm the man for the job!"

Dammit, Baxter, thought Harker; you're always a damn fool at times like this!

He crumpled the note and tossed it aside, and then he turned and headed back to the bridge. Captain Fuller, his first lieutenant, and the other senior officers had already come to a decision by the time Harker returned to them. The *Hood* would remain where it was until repairs could be made, which was not expected to take more than a few hours, and then sail back to Kingston. Fuller saw no other options, as they had no idea where their foe may have gone, and Harker did not feel that he was in any position to argue the matter. By nightfall, the battle cruiser was underway. They would sail back the way they had come, and they would consult the admiralty, and then return to their pursuit of the *Electric Shark*, should that be the course of action decided upon.

Chapter VI:
Plans Come Together

Billy Baxter sat shivering, crouching in a small storage closet somewhere aboard the *Electric Shark*. He shook his head in disbelief
and laughed to himself, amazed and relieved to be alive. He felt
fine, except for some bruises and the fact that he was soaking wet. He knew
that Harker would be shaking his head when he found that note, half in
anger, half in worry, but Baxter was damned proud of what he had done.
He just hoped he could do the rest of what he wanted to do, and not die in
the process. He stood up, the seawater still dripping from his clothes. He
opened the closet door, just a crack, and peeked out into the corridor of
the strange ship within which he now found himself. The immediate area
seemed to be empty, but he could hear voices in the distance, the voices
of men giving and responding to orders. He could tell by the tone of the
voices that it was shipboard business, but the words were foreign to him;
he did not know French.

He listened for a few minutes, until he finally heard the sound of
footsteps approaching his position. He had managed to sneak aboard the
ship by guiding his small lifeboat close to it and then climbing up the
outer hull, gaining access to the interior through a small opening on the
side. He had not yet seen any of the crew of the vessel. He did not know
what these "pirates," as he kept thinking of them, looked like. He had
decided that his first task had to be to determine whether or not they wore
some sort of uniform. He listened as the footsteps grew louder and the
source of the sound grew closer to where he hid.

Billy Baxter had never been a man of deep thought. He was more the sort of man who relied upon instinct; he was a man of action, not contemplation. He stood in that small supply closet, fists clenched, ready to strike if need be.

He heard the sound of boots tapping along the corridor floor, the lone person coming closer, closer. Finally, he was able to see the approaching man through the slightly open door. It was a young man, perhaps twenty-five, dressed in a gray outfit; shirt and trousers with black boots, certainly a ship's uniform of some kind. Baxter knew that if he was to be able to move about the ship he would need such clothing. As the man passed, Baxter swung the door open suddenly, slamming it into the pirate sailor, stunning him with the impact. The sailor reeled; Baxter stepped out of the hiding place and slammed a thick fist into the sailor's jaw! Another punch and the sailor fell unconscious like a light that had just been switched off! Baxter dragged the man into the closet, took the drab gray uniform for himself, and used his own clothes as rope, to tie the fallen pirate up and gag him. Then Baxter left the storage room, hoping his disguise would be sufficient, and hoping that the crew was large enough that they would not all recognize each other and detect a stranger among their number.

For all of his adult life, Baxter had been a soldier, first in Her Majesty's army and then as the personal assistant to Captain Harker. His battles had always been fought on land, so he knew little of shipboard business. Now's as good a time as any to learn the ways of the sea, Billy, old boy, he thought to himself as he began to explore the belly of *The Electric Shark*.

He passed two sailors in that corridor, nodded in acknowledgement of their presence, and was relieved when they only nodded back. He breathed a sigh of relief and kept going. As he went on, he could hear the pair exchange a few words, and realized that those two were not speaking French, but German! Good, thought Baxter to himself; this crew speaks various languages. That meant two things to him. First, it would not necessarily mean that he would be expected to speak the same language as everyone he met. Second, perhaps he could find an English-speaker, and interrogate him if the opportunity presented itself. He continued down the halls of the ship, not quite sure of where he was headed.

The *HMS Hood* had reached Kingston. The few small repairs that had been needed were completed and the return trip to Jamaica had been traveled without incident. Upon arrival, Captains Fuller and Harker had disembarked. Harker had gone to the hotel to find his butler, Picky Pickover,

"He continued down the halls of the ship..."

and explained what had happened so far and where Billy Baxter had gone, or tried to go, as Harker was not certain whether his faithful friend was dead or alive, and the question weighed heavily upon his mind. Once Pickover had been thoroughly updated on the events at sea, the pair went to rendezvous with Fuller at the British bank. At the bank, the trio made its way upstairs to the office of the president, Roger Mason. Mason left the three alone there, closing the office door as he went out. Once Harker was satisfied that he, Fuller, and Pickover were alone and had sufficient privacy, he sat down behind Mason's desk, picked up the telephone, and called the London office of Colonel Thurman Sharpe. The phone rang twice and Harker heard the strong, steady voice of his commanding officer answer.

"I'm going to assume that's you, Harker. I'm already aware of what happened out there in the Caribbean. Don't ask how, but I have sources. Now we have to decide where we go from here. Do you have any ideas at all, Captain?"

The line went silent for a moment as Harker thought. Finally, he spoke again.

"Give me twenty-four hours, Colonel. I don't have anything that I'm quite ready to suggest just yet. Perhaps we'll get lucky and someone, somewhere in the world will spot that ship and give us a tip…though I doubt we'll be that lucky twice. I just hope we can get to that Frenchman and stop him before he strikes again. We're lucky no one's been killed so far! I'll call you tomorrow, Sir."

Billy Baxter had spent the day exploring the lower decks of *The Electric Shark*. He had seen the engine rooms, the crew quarters, various storage areas and had even managed to take a glance into the empty sick bay. The interior of the ship was impressive and although he knew little about oceangoing vessels, he could tell that the design of the ship was nothing like that of anything used by the navies of the modern world. He wondered, in awe, where this amazing ship had come from. He encountered few sailors in the spacious lower decks and had no trouble as those he saw seemed too busy going about their tasks to question his presence there. Occasionally, orders or other information would be loudly barked over the ship's loudspeaker system, but Baxter rarely understood what he heard as it was usually in French.

Once he had had his fill of the bowels of the ship, he tried to gather the courage to venture up to the higher areas of the vessel. He steeled himself for whatever might lie ahead and found his way to the nearest ladder to the next highest deck. He climbed up and found himself in a corridor much like the one he had been in below. For the next few hours, he walked the halls, peered into those rooms that happened to have opened doors, and witnessed various crewmen going about their business. As he explored, he memorized the layout of the ship, his mind working much like it had during the war when he had committed the particulars of the land to memory in preparation for leading his squad of men into combat.

As he roamed the halls of the great and mysterious ship, Baxter stopped in front of one of the many rooms and looked inside. In the room was a single man, dressed in the uniform typical of all the vessel's crewmen. He was seated in front of a console of strange instruments; buttons, switches and levers of different shapes and sizes were attached to the panels before the man. Baxter stood in the doorway, undetected; trying to figure out exactly what he was looking at. He watched as the man manipulated the controls, twisting a lever, and then pressing a series of buttons, each of which had a single digit number below it. After the sequence of numbers had been punched, the man lifted a piece of apparatus, attached to the panel by a wire, to his face and began to speak into it. The English language came from the man's mouth, a most welcome sound to Billy Baxter's ears, for it meant that he could listen and understand!

"Yes, dear," said the crewman, in the tone of voice that a man takes on when talking to his wife, "I'll be home when I get home, and no, I don't know precisely when that'll be, but this job will put a nice bunch of pennies in our pockets; that much is for sure!"

Watching and listening in amazement, Baxter realized what he was witnessing. The man was talking by something very much like a telephone! In fact, Baxter guessed, the man's wife probably *was* using a telephone on her end of the conversation! How was this possible, Baxter asked himself? As far as he knew, telephones worked by wires, and there could be no wires connecting this device to the other telephone, so far out at sea were they. But Baxter trusted his senses and he knew that he was indeed witnessing an extraordinary sort of communications device. If this machine worked just like a telephone, and could be used to connect to other telephones many miles away, perhaps he could use it to reach Captain Harker!

Baxter considered the idea and decided that it was a valid one. Still, that was not the time to make his move. Before he could attempt to contact Harker, he had to find a way to determine where upon the vast seas of the world they were. Without a location to report, communication was useless and he certainly wasn't going to go to the trouble of calling the captain simply to say "hello!"

Angus McKay, now the second in command of *The Electric Shark*, answering only to "Admiral" Goulet himself, did not speak French. Therefore, when Goulet spoke to him, he used English. Now the two highest ranking officers aboard the ancient, powerful pirate vessel sat in Goulet's cabin, drinking coffee and discussing the next step in their quest for power and wealth.

"I tell you, McKay," spoke Pierre Goulet, "I am tired of minor acts of terror and piracy! Taking the money of that British bank was enjoyable, I suppose, but I wish to make a real mark upon the world! I find myself longing to impress upon this world just how potent a weapon this vessel truly is. Soon, my friend, the world will quake in fear at the very mention of this, my *Electric Shark* and I, its master!"

McKay said nothing, knowing that it was not a good idea to interrupt one of Goulet's mad rants. He simply let the admiral continue.

"I have supreme confidence in this great sailing weapon that is at our disposal. Now, my friend, we will demonstrate our power in a manner that will show the entire world that we are a force to be feared! To the Atlantic Ocean we shall now sail, and into the English channel. We shall position ourselves in that narrow portion of the channel where we can be near to both England and France, sitting between Dover and Calais. From there, we can travel between one city and the other, and within a short period of time launch strikes against both nations, demonstrating that even two of the most powerful nations on this Earth are no match for us. Let the British navy come against us once more, let the French also try to strike us down! Let them come! I shall not hesitate to sink the ships of either nation. The English have ruled the seas for far too long, and the French, though they are the nation into which I was born, I owe no loyalty to, either. By terrorizing both those great kingdoms, I shall show the world that I am to be its new master!"

With that final outburst of pompous joy, Goulet poured the last of his coffee down his throat and slammed the empty mug down on his desk. He stood up from his chair, his chest puffed out in a show of utter confidence. McKay stood too; ready to follow his commander to the bridge.

"Come, McKay," said Goulet. "We have preparations to make! In thirty days, both England and France will bow to us!"

As they left the cabin and stormed down the corridor of the ship, neither of them paid any attention to the sailor whom they passed in the hall. Why would they? He was just one of the many crewmen who served aboard *The Electric Shark*.

As the French megalomaniac and his first officer hurried by, Billy Baxter, disguised in the drab gray shirt and trousers of the vessel's personnel, smiled. Now he knew the pirates' plans. Now he had to get that information to the proper authorities.

Baxter, once the coast was clear, ran down the halls of the ship, climbed down to one deck below, and returned to the room where he had seen the communications man using that strange telephone device to call his wife in what Baxter assumed was England. He did not waste any time with subtlety as there were no other crewmen in sight. He entered the radio room through its open door. The radio operator turned around at the sound of Baxter's approach. Baxter, not stopping to think or strategize, pounced! He threw himself at the radio man, slamming into him and upsetting the balance of his chair. Baxter's thick fist crashed into the radio man's jaw and the sailor was knocked out cold. Baxter tossed the unconscious body aside, closed the door behind him, and sat down in the now vacant chair. Thinking back to how he had previously seen the man operate the communications apparatus, he began to manipulate the controls. He picked up the mouthpiece and held it to his face. He pressed a small green button on the console. The voice of a female operator came into his ear. The voice was that of a young woman with a slight accent, possibly Dutch.

"Good day," the woman said in accented English. "Would you like to place a call?"

Baxter paused. He knew what he wanted to do, but did not know how to get the number that he wanted to call. Then he remembered something. He reached into his pocket. He had transferred the contents of his pockets from his own clothing into the stolen uniform. He hoped that the item he needed was still with him and had not come out when he had left his lifeboat to climb aboard the ship. In a second, he had found it; a matchbook he had acquired in the hotel in Kingston. It was soaked and crumbling, but the lettering on the book of matches was still, just barely, legible. He read the number for the hotel lobby from the matchbook to the woman on the line.

"One moment, Sir." said the operator.

Baxter heard a ringing; once, twice, three times, and then the sound of a telephone being answered.

"Kingston Plaza Hotel," said another voice, this one male, with the distinctive tone of someone who had lived in Jamaica for many years. "How can I be of service today?"

Baxter grinned. His plan was working.

"Captain Quincy Harker," he said.

The line rang again. Baxter hoped his captain had returned to the hotel after the confrontation between *The Electric Shark* and *HMS Hood*.

In his suite at the Kingston Plaza Hotel, Quincy Harker had just lit a cigarette. He was sitting cross-legged on the bed, eyes closed, blocking out all sights and sounds, limiting his awareness to the scent and taste of the tobacco, and the workings of his sharp mind. He was thinking of the awesome power of the Frenchman's ship, and pondering how to best combat such a threat. He was certain, having seen *The Electric Shark*'s power firsthand, that no vessel in the British fleet could withstand it. Could a vast armada be assembled to track down the pirates, perhaps there was some chance of victory, but that would take time, and Harker feared that the enemy would strike again before too long, though he did not know where. There had to be a way. He had one idea, simmering in the back of his mind, but it was a long shot. He knew of a ship, or what had once been a ship, that was just as strange and unusually equipped as the pirate vessel, but getting it into action would not be easy. Even if that could be done, he still had to know where the Frenchman and his pirates would be. How could he possibly locate them, for all the vastness of the seas, before it was too late to prevent another attack?

Just as those thoughts and questions swirled around in Harker's busy mind, there was a knock on his door. He opened his eyes, put his cigarette in the bedside ashtray, stood, and walked over to the door. He opened it to find one of the hotel's red-uniformed bellhops standing there.

"Captain Harker?" said the boy, "there's a call for you in the lobby, Sir. It seems to be most urgent. It's a Sergeant Baxter, I think they said."

Harker didn't say anything to the bellhop. He didn't tip the lad or thank him. He just rushed past him, flew through the door to the stairwell, and bounded down to the lobby, several steps at a time.

"Billy? Billy, is that you?" Harker asked as he put the telephone receiver to his ear. "Where are you? What? You're still on that ship? But how are you calling here from the middle of the ocean? Oh. I see. That's amazing! What? The English Channel; oh, Hell! When? Thirty days! All right, Baxter, you've done a damn brave thing, Sergeant! Now get out of that room and find a place to hide and stay put! Don't do anything stupid!"

Harker heard the line click as Baxter, many miles away, ended the conversation. Harker could have stood there for an hour, his mind wandering in awe of the capabilities of that ship's communication systems, but he did not. He nodded thanks to the clerk at the desk, put down the telephone, turned and entered one of the booths against the wall of the lobby. He did not like to make official calls where he could be heard. He had just broken that rule, out of necessity, when it came to Baxter's call, but he needed a bit of privacy now. He closed the phone booth door behind him and picked up the phone. Within minutes, he was connected to the office of his superior officer in London.

"Colonel Sharpe here," barked the voice in Harker's ear.

"Listen, Colonel," Harker said back to him, "I don't have time to explain this, but I need something from you. Please don't hesitate; thousands of lives might depend on it! Those pirates are going to head for the English Channel in a month, and they plan on hitting both Dover and Calais! What I need, Colonel is authorization to borrow the *Hood*. Let me take her on a little trip, Sir. I've no time to explain my plan now, but it may be our only hope of beating that lunatic Frenchman at this game of his. Can I take the *Hood*, Sir?"

Colonel Sharpe did not hesitate. Many past experiences had taught him to trust Captain Harker.

"All right, Harker," Sharpe answered, "but work with Captain Fuller, not against him. You haven't exactly got a lot of nautical experience. Now get moving and whatever you're up to had better be the answer to this mess."

The colonel hung up, Harker got moving. In twenty minutes, Quincy Harker and Picky Pickover were boarding the *HMS Hood*.

Chapter VII:
Legends of the Sea

Billy Baxter had just completed his short but vitally important call to Captain Harker when he heard the ominous sound of the door to the communications room opening behind him.

"Raise your hands and turn slowly around!" barked a heavily accented, probably German, voice.

Baxter did as told, putting his hands up and rotating in the spot where he stood. He turned to face two armed men, dressed like the other crewmen of the ship.

"I don't know you or why you are here…but you are clearly an intruder!" one of the armed sailors said as he looked at the unconscious radioman on the floor to Baxter's right. "Come with us. The admiral will want to see you. Perhaps he will have us kill you. Now walk!"

Baxter continued to do as he was told. He was unarmed and outnumbered.

The *HMS Hood* was already out at sea, having sailed from Kingston as soon as Harker and Pickover had boarded. Harker politely, but firmly, gave Captain David Fuller a certain password, which indicated that he now had the authority to command the movements of the Hood. Fuller did not completely like handing the reigns of the ship over to a non-naval officer, but he had gotten along well with Harker so far and predicted that the two captains would get along amicably.

Once they were underway, Harker sent Pickover to place their bags in the cabins they would use while on board. Fuller left the first lieutenant in charge of the bridge and relocated to his quarters, joined by Harker. Fuller offered Harker some tea, but the offer was declined.

"All right, Harker," said Captain Fuller, "my ship is at your disposal, but at least clue me in on where we're heading."

Harker gestured towards the chair that stood in the corner of the cabin.

"You should sit down, Captain. This is going to be an odd conver-sation."

Fuller sat down as Harker had suggested. Harker began to speak.

"Captain Fuller, I know how to find a ship that just might be capable of defeating the one possessed by that French pirate! Tell me, Fuller; have you ever read the works of Jules Verne?"

Fuller nodded; surprised that Harker had brought up the name of a writer of fantastic fiction.

"Yes, yes I have. I suppose many boys who grow up to be sailing men read *Twenty Thousand Leagues* when they were young. Why do you ask?"

Harker laughed as he began to explain his reasoning.

"Well, Captain, it may surprise you to hear this, but Verne didn't base all of his books entirely on the contents of his imagination. If you look into some of the things I've looked into in my life, you might find that small kernels of truth, strange truth, can be found in the most unexpected of places.

"You see, Fuller, while a great deal of what was in that book, as well as Verne's other books, was pure fiction, the idea of that great submarine of Nemo's, The *Nautilus*, came from a real vessel, called by that very name. Large chunks of that novel, as well as one of Verne's other books, the sequel *The Mysterious Island*, are based on true events!

"Here, my friend is the truth, so far as I know it. Now is neither the time nor the place to explain how I came to this knowledge, but suffice it to say that my work for Her Majesty's government has enabled me to learn many things that would surprise you.

"There really was a man like the one whom Verne called 'Captain Nemo' in his books. This man truly did possess a great and most unusual ship, which he did indeed call the *Nautilus*! Unlike the character in those books, the real Nemo did not build the ship himself. Rather, he found it, much as I believe our French pirate, Pierre Goulet, found his *Electric Shark*. What Nemo believed, what Jules Verne believed, and what I believe, is that the *Nautilus*, and probably the *Electric Shark* as well, are remnants of some ancient and vastly more advanced civilization that once dwelt upon the Earth and sailed her seas. Perhaps the two great vessels are even artifacts of the fabled continent of Atlantis! Whatever their origins, I suspect that the two ships may be of the same source. Perhaps, just as the best way to crack the shells of walnuts is to press them against each other, the *Nautilus* may be our best and perhaps only chance of defeating Goulet and his *Shark*!"

David Fuller's head was spinning. He had not expected to be hearing this, of all things, from the mouth of Quincy Harker.

"Assuming you're correct, Captain Harker, how would we even find this *Nautilus*, and would it still be operational? Verne wrote his books decades ago and he ended *The Mysterious Island*, if I recall correctly, with the ship being scuttled and serving as the tomb of Captain Nemo!"

Harker nodded.

"That is indeed the case, Captain Fuller, but I happen to know the location where the remains of the *Nautilus* lie. If the information I have is accurate, we just might be able to reach that place and then we shall see if we can resurrect that ship before it's too late to put and end to Goulet's madness!

"And one other thing, Fuller; this is the key of the matter. Verne, in his writings, actually downplayed the capabilities of the ship for fear that a more accurate depiction would be difficult for the minds of readers in the 1870s to understand. As potent a seafaring weapon as the Nautilus was on paper, I have high hopes that it is much, much more interesting in reality. I only hope that it has not fallen into too great a state of disrepair for us to salvage it."

Fuller had his doubts, but he had to admit that he was intrigued by the story he had just heard.

"Back to the bridge, then," Fuller suggested. "I'm assuming you have coordinates for our helm."

Side by side, the two captains trekked back up to the command center of the *HMS Hood*.

Far, far away from the bridge of that British battle cruiser, aboard the *Electric Shark*, Billy Baxter stood before Pierre Goulet. The crewmen who had found Baxter in the communications room had brought him to their commander. Now they stood in Goulet's cabin, behind Baxter, their guns still aimed at his back, as the retired sergeant of the British Army faced the master of the mighty vessel on which he was now a helpless stowaway.

"What is your name?" Goulet demanded to know, growling at Baxter in his French-accented English.

"Billy Baxter, sergeant, retired, British Army!" Baxter snapped back.

"What are you doing on my ship?" Goulet questioned him loudly.

"Making sure you don't do any more harm, you lousy pirate!" Baxter shouted.

Goulet laughed and mocked him.

"You stupid English; one man comes to fight against the entire crew of the greatest ship ever to sail the seas! How foolish can you be?"

Baxter, never one to let a bit of fear lessen his ability to tell it like he saw it, went right back at Goulet.

"You just wait, you scoundrel! The Hound Dog will come…and you'll be wishin' you never set sail in this garbage scow to begin with!"

That was enough for Pierre Goulet.

"Throw him in the brig; the solitary cell!" he ordered his men, and he left the room as they led Baxter away, forcibly.

Two weeks had passed since the call had come from the *Electric Shark* to the hotel in Kingston, warning Harker of Goulet's plan to sail into the English Channel. For the entire fortnight, the *HMS Hood* had been racing at full speed to the site of the coordinates given to the navigator by Harker. They had made it to the South Pacific and were nearing the area where the small island they sought was expected to be found.

Quincy Harker stood on the deck of the *Hood*, smoking a cigarette. Captain Fuller and Picky Pickover were with him. They watched a lush, green island grow closer and closer as they approached it.

"We must swing around to the western side of the island, Captain," said Harker. "Once there, we should find that we can sail up to the mouth of a series of caves. A ship the size of ours is much too wide to enter those caverns. We shall have to leave the *Hood* and use a smaller boat, one of your lifeboats, to go in and search for that which we seek."

Not more than thirty minutes later, a small boat was indeed moving away from the British warship and moving towards the western shores of the unnamed Pacific island. The boat contained Quincy Harker, David Fuller, and Sergeant Major Craig of the *Hood*'s company of Royal Marines. Harker's butler, Pickover, had wanted to go along as well, so strong was his loyalty to Harker, but his master had ordered him to stay aboard the battle cruiser. Pickover was a good friend, but sometimes faint of heart, and Harker had enough to worry about.

They reached the island quickly enough and rowed along until they saw just what Harker had predicted they would find; a black and shadowy opening in the walls of the hills that stood on the western shore. None aboard the small boat wanted to hesitate; they plowed along, moving through the waters, right into the gaping mouth that stretched open before them. As they left daylight, Sgt. Maj. Craig lit the battery powered searchlight which they had brought along. The cavern, and the wide stream within looked much as one would expect them to; dark waters below, craggy, stalagmite ceiling above. None of the men spoke as they moved along, not sure if any natives, hostile or otherwise inhabited the island. While there was no one in sight, they thought the caves, with likely echoes, might amplify their voices, with potentially negative results. The minutes ticked by and they saw no sign of any activity whatsoever.

On and on they sailed in that little boat; surprised that the stream never did narrow or grow shallow, but continued on unchangingly. An hour passed. Finally, they could see the tunnel begin to widen a bit, then a bit more. Then, so suddenly that it caught them all, experienced sailor, intelligence officer, and hardened marine alike, off guard, it opened into a much wider cave!

"Good lord!" said Captain Fuller, the first to find words as the tunnel suddenly widened tremendously and the light of the sergeant major's lamp reflected off of the amazing object that sat, funereally still, in the waters of that long neglected cave!

"You were right, Harker!" Fuller shouted, forgetting the precautionary silence.

"It's beautiful!" said Sgt. Maj. Craig, clearly impressed by what he saw.

Quincy Harker chuckled. He was not a conceited man by any stretch, but he was tremendously amused by the fact that his hopes had paid off.

"Gentlemen," he said with joy, "I give you…the *Nautilus*!"

Chapter VIII:
Setting Sail

The *Nautilus* was not a huge ship, much shorter and narrower than a battle cruiser like the *Hood,* but still large enough to impress those who were seeing it for the first time. It was not so much its size that made such an impression though, but its sleek and elegant beauty, resembling a long cylinder with fins and apertures like one might expect to see on some rare breed of exotic fish. It looked as much like some unique work of art as it looked like a fearsome seafaring vessel.

Captain Fuller was clearly enthused by the sight of such a ship.

"What are we waiting for?" shouted the British mariner. "Let's get closer and see if we can get aboard the thing!"

Harker nodded in agreement and the small lifeboat moved closer and closer to the hulking artifact before them. Soon, they were right up alongside the *Nautilus*. Sgt. Maj. Craig stayed in the boat to make certain that it did not drift away. Fuller and Harker eagerly climbed up the side of the legendary vessel's hull, gripping the strange fin-like pieces that jutted out and pulling them up. Luckily, both men were in excellent physical condition. They stood atop the ship and looked around them. There was a small hatch there, not unlike those found on most submarines; the two captains stared at it, trying to figure out a way to open it and gain entrance to the ancient ship. Harker knelt down near the hatch and touched its handle.

Not hesitating a bit, the hatch suddenly slid open, requiring no physical manipulation at all! Harker and Fuller were stunned, but took full advantage of the pleasant surprise and entered through the opening, Harker going first, then Fuller. They descended down into the darkness, but it did not remain dark for long as electrical lights switched on, almost as if the ship had a sort of mechanical sentience and was able to sense the arrival of occupants.

The captains looked around, taking in the sight of cold steel walls decorated with levers, buttons and mechanisms of obviously unusual design. It truly felt to both Harker and Fuller as if they had entered another time and world. They excitedly made their way to the front of the vessel, finding more instruments and two comfortable looking chairs which were obviously there for the ship's navigation and helm operators to occupy.

Fuller sat down at one of the chairs. He lightly touched one of the control levers. He and Harker jumped, startled, when the hum of machinery at work suddenly became audible. Even more stunning to them was the fact that the ship suddenly began to speak to them!

"Greetings...and welcome aboard the *Nautilus*! If you have found this vessel and gained access to this, its bridge, then I congratulate you. I, during life, was known as Nemo...Captain Nemo to some! This was my ship, a ship I did not build, but found; a ship which I believe to be a relic of some long forgotten society, many centuries more advanced than the one into which I was born! This ship had been kind to me...as I hope its future masters shall be kind to it. It took me many months of trial and error to learn to utilize the many wonders of which this vessel is capable. As I neared the end of my life, I made some small alterations to the *Nautilus*, in the hopes that such changes would make the process of learning simpler for those who might one day become its captains. Perhaps many years have passed since my death, but I live on in this recording of my voice, to welcome to this ship any who may come after me. In life, I was a harsh commander, a strict master, and perhaps an enigma to most who encountered me. I regret none of what I did in life, yet I find that now, as I near my inevitable death, I wish to give something to those who, like me, choose a life upon...and beneath...the oceans of this Earth! I wish you good fortune, my fellow mariners. May history be kind to all of us!"

Harker and Fuller sat there for many minutes, both silent and at a loss for words. They were in awe, having just been privileged to hear the voice of a nautical legend. Finally, Quincy Harker broke the long silence.

"Stay here, Fuller. I'll go call Sergeant Craig aboard. I don't think we'll need that little lifeboat anymore!"

Billy Baxter sat, as he had for many days, so many that he had lost count of them, on the floor of the little solitary cell into which he had been unceremoniously deposited by the crewmen of the *Electric Shark*.

Twice a day, a bowl of rancid tasting gruel and a small cup of water were shoved in through a small panel in the otherwise solid cell door. When not consuming his two cruel meals, Baxter simply sat there, never giving up hope that his salvation would come, in the form of his friend and commander, Captain Quincy "Hound Dog" Harker. His face dirty and decorated with what had grown into thick stubble, Baxter could do nothing but wait.

Once Craig had come aboard the *Nautilus*, Harker had rejoined Fuller on the bridge and the pair had set to work trying to learn how to operate the strange ship and determine how well maintained the ship still was after decades of abandonment. Surprisingly, all the ship's advanced systems seemed to be functional, which relieved the captains greatly, as it was doubtful that even the best modern engineers would be able to repair such a mysterious vessel. Soon, Fuller and Harker had figured out the basics of the helm and the great ship smoothly sailed out of the deep cavern and into the sunlight and blue sea once more. From the deck of the *HMS Hood* came loud cheers and jubilant applause as the *Nautilus* came into view.

Fuller called all of his senior officers over from the battle cruiser to have a quick look at the mighty ship they had found in that hidden cavern. All the men were awed by what they saw within. A conference was held, including the *Hood*'s officers and Captain Harker. It was decided that the *Nautilus*, due to its advanced nature and the fact that it could, apparently, almost run itself, would need only a small crew.

Fuller and Harker would command the *Nautilus* together, leaving the first lieutenant in command of the British ship. Joining the new crew of Nemo's old vessel would be Sgt. Maj. Craig and twenty of his Royal Marines, the *Hood*'s chief engineer, navigation officer, surgeon, and an assortment of twelve sailors. Picky Pickover also insisted on coming aboard to sail beside Captain Harker. The *Nautilus* would sail at top speed, a speed which was yet to be discovered, to the English Channel, to await the arrival and attempted attack of the *Electric Shark*. *HMS Hood* would also set course for that place and eventually rendezvous with Fuller, Harker and the others, although all present assumed that the *Hood*'s trip would be a longer, slower one. Once the crew had boarded the *Nautilus* and sufficient provisions had been brought aboard, the mighty ship from the depths of the past began to cruise away from the small island in the South Pacific where it had slept for nearly half a century.

"From the deck of the HMS Hood came loud cheers..."

Chapter IX:
Fire on the Water

Over the next two weeks, Harker, Fuller, and their small crew of thirty-five men learned the methods of operating the amazing warship that had come into their possession. Fuller and the navigator learned to sail the ship across the seas of the world. The engineer learned how to keep up the ship's maintenance. Harker oversaw the whole process, and the other sailors aboard learned their tasks quickly and efficiently. Soon enough, the *Nautilus* was once again able to submerge or surface at the will of its personnel; the weapons systems had been tested on small, uninhabited islands, and the various systems of the ship had, more or less, been figured out. The *Nautilus* sped along, sailing at full speed for most of the journey, until it reached the English Channel. Submerging and waiting, the ancient vessel sat and waited for the battle that every man on board expected to come at any moment. Quincy Harker, as always, was ready for action, and willing to do whatever it would take to win. First and foremost in his thoughts was the defense of his own country, England, and also of France. Not far behind his primary concern was his deep feeling of worry about his friend, his old sergeant, Billy Baxter. He hoped he would be able to find a way to both sink the *Electric Shark*, and save his old friend.

It had been a quiet morning aboard the *Nautilus*. The ship waited, submerged, beneath the mostly calm waters of the English Channel. The navigator had been left in charge while Harker and Fuller had gone to the small but nicely equipped dining area to play a friendly game of cards, hoping to accelerate the hours before the inevitable clash with the pirate vessel whose arrival they awaited. Fuller was shuffling the deck as Harker was taking a long, deep drag on a freshly lit cigarette. Picky Pickover was just walking over with two glasses of wine for the captains, the butler having been delighted to find a fully stocked liquor supply among the *Nautilus's* many luxuries.

The wine glasses fell to the floor and shattered, the red liquid splattering the three men's shoes as Pickover was startled by a sudden, very loud, alarm! Harker and Fuller jumped to their feet. The poor butler was left to clean up the mess as the captains made their way to the bridge as fast as they could move.

Entering the bridge, they found sailors moving about, operating the strange machinery that had been new to them, unseen by them, only a few short weeks ago.

"Lieutenant...report!" barked Captain Fuller to the navigation officer, who answered calmly, but crisply, a characteristic way of speaking for almost all British naval officers.

"Captain, that sound is, apparently, a proximity alarm to warn us of the approach of any other ships. They've arrived, Sir. They're on the surface. I don't know if they're aware of our presence!"

His report given, the young officer got up from his chair and away from the periscope through which he had been peering, making room there for the captain. He then sat down in the other control chair, his hands ready to see to his duties, ready to follow any order that Fuller saw fit to give.

Fuller settled into his now open seat, leaned forward and looked into the periscope. "It's up there, all right," he said. "I don't think it sees us; at least not yet."

On the water's surface, Pierre Goulet and Angus McKay stood out on the open deck of the *Electric Shark*. Goulet was grinning in a wicked smile, full of pompous confidence.

"Here we sit, McKay," the French pirate began to brag, "between two of the most powerful nations ever to exist on this planet...yet how England and France must both pale in comparison to the might and ingenuity of whatever great empire it was that built vessels of war such as the one that now belongs to me! In moments now, McKay, these two great nations shall tremble at the fury of the force and fire which shall rain down upon them from the guns of the *Electric Shark*!

"Look around us, McKay!" gloated Goulet, his hands held high in a gesture of arrogance as he spun around on the ship's deck. "On one side of us, the White Cliffs of Dover, a landmark as symbolic of England as Westminster Abbey or Big Ben; on the other side, the French coast, the town of Calais! Which shall it be, McKay? Which nations shall fear us first! Let it be France, the nation which gave birth to the sea's greatest warrior! Your admiral returns to you, oh France. I return to rule over you!"

Goulet grabbed a small device which was part of the ship's advanced equipment. It was a sort of microphone, connecting his voice from atop the ship with the men under his command who sat inside the ship's control room, awaiting his orders.

"Helm," he spat, "take us closer to the French side of the Channel!"

Inside the *Nautilus*, Captain Fuller turned his gaze from the periscope and momentarily turned to his partner-in-command.

"Harker, they're moving in towards Calais. They're preparing to attack, I think!"

Quincy Harker did not hesitate, his bravery rising to the surface.

"We can't let them even begin an assault. One innocent injured is one too many. I vote that we surface and give them a warning."

Fuller agreed. If the two captains had one thing in common, it was an absolute fearlessness when duty called.

"Surface, surface!" the British sea captain ordered his men.

Reacting to a tremendously loud sound, the sudden WHOOSH of large amounts of water shooting up, geyser-like, into the air, Pierre Goulet and Angus McKay turned around to behold the sight of the *Nautilus* appearing from beneath the waves.

"My God," McKay blurted out, "it's another ship, just like ours!"

"Who dares..." Goulet began to cry out, before being interrupted by the booming voice coming from the loudspeaker apparatus of the newly arrived vessel. It was an English voice, Goulet could tell immediately.

"Pierre Goulet and crew of the *Electric Shark*, this is Captain David Fuller of the *HMS Nautilus*! You are trespassing in waters shared by the British Empire and the people of France. You will surrender immediately and prepare to be boarded. You have been given fair warning. Comply or we shall be forced to open fire!"

It only took a moment for the reply to come across the air between the two ancient vessels.

"So...the British have found the legendary ship of Nemo! It will be of no help to you. I am Admiral Pierre Goulet. You shall not be forced to open fire. You shall be forced to sink!"

Through the wide bridge window of the *Nautilus*, Captain Fuller watched the gun hatches on the deck of the *Electric Shark* slide open, the small cannons emerging and beginning to glow with the eerie light of antediluvian war machines.

"Brace for impact!" he shouted to his crew. Those who were seated held fast to the arms of their chairs. Others grabbed hold of railings. Quincy Harker grasped the back of Fuller's chair as he stood directly behind his friend, watching the spectacle through the same window.

Blasts of energy shot forth from the enemy vessel…and fizzled out of existence midway between the originating guns and the hull of their intended target!

On the *Electric Shark*, Pierre Goulet cursed, incredulous.

On the *Nautilus*, David Fuller smiled, but did not understand.

"What the hell?" Fuller said in shock, "there was no impact, nothing at all! What happened?"

Quincy Harker hazarded a guess.

"I can think of an explanation," he said, speaking as quickly as the theory came to him. "Perhaps this is yet another example of the builders of these ships' amazing technology. We might assume that these two vessels were once part of the same fleet. Perhaps their weapons were designed in such a way as to prevent them from firing, intentionally or accidentally, upon each other. Perhaps these two ships are immune to each others' guns!"

Fuller, clearly willing to entertain Harker's idea, called out his next order.

"We'll test that theory of yours, Captain Harker! Gunnery men, fire at will!"

The gun hatches of the *Nautilus* slid open and bolts of blue light flew forth…only to vanish as suddenly as the attack of the pirate ship had been nullified.

On the *Electric Shark*, Goulet and McKay had gone below, back to the bridge, to better run the battle. As they watched the British attack against them fail, Goulet decided their course of action.

"It seems to be a stalemate, though I do not understand why! Forget the English then! Weapons officer, fire on Calais!"

On the bridge of the *Nautilus*, Fuller saw what the *Electric Shark* was about to do.

"They're about to fire on the French! What can we do? Full maneuvering speed! Bring us up next to them!"

The *Nautilus* moved forward with a sudden burst of speed, slicing through the water, pulling up right alongside the *Electric Shark*.

"I'm giving them a little tap," said Fuller as he manipulated the helm controls.

There was a great scraping noise, like fingernails trailing down a chalkboard, as the two thick metal hulls rubbed against each other. Both ships shook. Fuller's maneuver had apparently surprised the men aboard Goulet's ship, for the *Electric Shark*'s guns failed to fire on the little French coastal town.

"Sergeant Major Craig," said Fuller, calling out to the leader of the Royal Marines aboard the *Nautilus*, "I think it's time to board that ship!"

"Right away, Sir!" said the tough veteran. He pressed a button on the control console, enabling him to be heard on every deck of the ship. "All marines gather on deck immediately; all marines on deck at once!"

He ran up onto the ship's outer deck, his pistol already in hand; ready to lead his men in a leaping charge from one ship to the other.

Quincy Harker pulled his own pistol from his belt and began to follow just behind Sergeant Major Craig.

"Fuller, good luck here! I'm going in with the marines! My friend is over there and I aim to find him before we sink or shoot all those pirate bastards!"

In moments, Harker, Craig and twenty Royal Marines were on deck, all armed, and ready to go into battle. The *Nautilus* swung towards the *Electric Shark* again, just close enough to tickle the hull. As the ships briefly scraped together one more time, Craig gave the order and the entire unit of marines ran and jumped from one deck to the other. As they arrived on the deck of the pirate ship, armed thugs from Goulet's crew, led by Angus McKay, swarmed out from below. Men met hand to hand if they were close enough, grappling and wrestling on the deck. Others opened fire and bullets flew. It was utter chaos atop the *Electric Shark*!

Quincy Harker made his way through the crowd and the din of battle. He knew the marines could handle themselves under the capable leadership of Sergeant Major Craig. He had one task on his mind that he had to try to complete. He had to find Billy Baxter, if the old warrior was even still alive. He would get below deck as quickly as possible and hope to find out where Baxter was before he got himself killed! Down one of the ladders he slid, landing in a hallway, almost getting himself run over by a frantic crewman who ran right past him, apparently not realizing that Harker was an intruder. Harker ran the way the pirate had come from, seeing a door in front of him and figuring it to be as good a way to begin his search as any. He flew through the door, which opened automatically at his approach…and found himself on the ship's bridge, face to face with a man who could only have been the lead pirate himself, "Admiral" Pierre Goulet! The Frenchman was furiously trying to exert control over his crewmen, all of whom seemed to be fleeing the bridge to try to get up on deck and join the brawl.

Harker aimed his pistol at Goulet, who was standing in front of one of the many control panels on the bridge.

"Put your hands up…Admiral," Harker ordered him with unmistakable sarcasm behind his words.

Goulet started to raise his hands, but it was a feigned surrender. He intentionally fell backwards, striking a control lever as he moved. The ship lurched to one side and Harker lost his balance, his gun flying from his grip, hitting the floor, and sliding right into the possession of Goulet. The French pirate picked up the gun, fired once at Harker, missing! Harker, however, ducked and slid while trying to avoid the shot, was thrown off balance momentarily, and could not tackle Goulet before the Frenchman disappeared around the corner and out of sight. Dammit, Harker thought, I'm unarmed and the bastard's still loose!

Harker got up, brushed himself off, and continued on his way. He ran down the next corridor he found and kept moving, glancing into each doorway he saw. There were no crew left down in the lower decks of the ship now, all of them having run up top, most of them giving in to fear and panic. They were, after all, just hired goons, not disciplined, trained military men like those who had served on the *Hood* and now on the *Nautilus*.

Harker could still hear bursts of gunfire and the sounds of hand to hand combat up above him. He could feel the ship rocking with the occasional impact of the *Nautilus* ramming up against it. He kept running, kept descending further into the bowels of the vessel.

Up on deck, the marines had mopped up most of the mess. A few of them had been killed or wounded, but overall the hired mercenaries of Goulet's crew were no match for the skilled, drilled veterans under Craig's command. Many of the pirates had fallen, a few had jumped overboard in a foolish escape attempt, and many more had thrown up their hands in surrender. Even the second in command of the *Electric Shark*, Angus McKay, had seen the folly of trying to fight on and he too had conceded defeat. The two massive, ancient vessels hovered there in the waters between England and France as Craig and his men directed the prisoners over to the *Nautilus*. Only the pirates' leader was unaccounted for.

Back in the belly of the *Electric Shark*, Pierre Goulet had decided what he was going to do. He would not let his magnificent ship fall into the hands of the British. To the engine room he ran. Using his knowledge of the ancient machinery, some of which knowledge he had not even shared with his most trusted minions, he locked the ship's gears so that the vessel could not move, no matter how much power was run into the engines. Then he turned the engines on at full power. He knew it would only be a matter of time before the immense power of that very old technology could no longer be contained while the ship was unmoving. When that moment came, the *Electric Shark* would tear itself to pieces...and perhaps take the *Nautilus* with it. His grim task completed, Goulet left the engine room. He was an "admiral," at least in his own mind, and unlike a mere "captain," had no intention of going down with his ship!

Moments later, Quincy Harker arrived in that very same engine room. Things learned during his weeks on the *Nautilus*, partnered with his keen observational skills, told him immediately that those engines could not withstand the accumulating pressure for much longer. He reached for the communications device that would usually be used to allow the engineers to talk to those on the bridge. As he picked up the telephone-like device, he hoped that the ship's loudspeaker was connected to the same line. He pressed the buttons and hoped, and then he spoke.

"Captain Fuller, listen to me! It's Harker! This ship is going to blow! Get the *Nautilus* out of here! Move quickly! I'm going to try for the escape boat; maybe there's one here like the one you have! We'll have drinks in Kingston next time we're both there! Now get going!"

On the *Nautilus*, Captain Fuller gave the order to sail away from the *Electric Shark* at best possible speed. He hated to leave Harker, who had quickly become his friend, behind, but he understood that his duty required that he protect the majority of his men before one individual. He turned to Picky Pickover, who had just arrived on the bridge, and mouthed the words, "I'm sorry."

Harker knew that since the two old warships were so similar in capabilities and equipment, there was a good chance that the *Electric Shark*, like the *Nautilus*, had a motorized escape boat hidden in its hull, a small craft big enough for several people, and fast enough to outrun the explosion of the vessel that housed it. But first, he knew, he had to make one last attempt at finding Baxter.

He ran down the one last corridor of the bottommost deck of the ship. He kicked open door after door, finally reaching the last one. He tried to turn the knob, but it was locked.

"Is anyone in there?" he shouted.

A faint whimper came from behind the door.

"Captain…ha! I told that rotten Frenchman you'd be along soon enough; told him the old Hound Dog would bite him were it hurts the most."

Harker smiled from ear to ear.

"Stand back, Sergeant; that's an order!" he said. He readied himself and he kicked that door with all the force he could muster. He smiled again as he heard the hinges crack. The door fell open and Billy Baxter, beaten, bruised, bearded and exhausted tumbled out of the cell, his eyes blinking and tearing as he confronted light for the first time in a month. He had just enough strength left to hobble along, supported by Harker.

As they walked, Harker trying to hurry Baxter along without pushing him too hard, they could feel the shaking of the ship worsening. It would not be long, Harker knew, before the engines burst at the seams, dooming anyone left on board. They had to make it to that escape boat.

Down one more corridor they travelled, finally spotting the place they sought. Harker opened the hatch to the little craft that would be their salvation. He shoved the semi-conscious Baxter inside and then followed him in. He closed the hatch behind them and prepared to push the lever that would jettison them from the main body of the *Electric Shark*.

"I knew I should have learned to operate this mechanism sooner," said the sudden voice of Pierre Goulet, the sound coming out of the shadows and startling Harker. The Hound Dog whirled around to see Goulet sitting there, aiming his gun right at Harker's chest.

"I should have…but I did not," Goulet continued, "and so here I sit, waiting for you, my enemy, to operate it for me. Help me escape this vessel alive…and perhaps I shall allow you two meddlers to live as well."

Harker was tired of playing the Frenchman's game. He had spent well over a month on a wild chase all over the globe because of the pirate admiral's greed. Enough was enough. To hell with the Frenchman's gun, Harker thought to himself. He punched the launching lever and the small escape boat flew forth from the hull of its mother ship and sped off into the English Channel.

The startled Pierre Goulet pulled the trigger, intending to put a bullet right into the heart of Quincy Harker! As the finger closed around the trigger, another arm swung forward, the nearly dead-tired Billy Baxter using his last ounce of energy to jar the pirate's gun hand just enough to throw off his aim. There was a loud "crack" as the gun fired, a sharp "ping" as the bullet ricocheted off the steel ceiling of the tiny boat...and a dull "chuff" as it embedded itself in the skull of the very man who had just fired it! Pierre Goulet, the man who had wanted nothing less that to rule the world by means of the sea, slumped forward where he sat. His game was over and he had lost.

The escape boat moved quickly away from the *Electric Shark*, and just in the nick of time. Behind the small boat, the larger vessel finally blew. Those lucky enough to be up upon the cliffs of Dover on that day, and those lucky enough to be on the coast of Calais on that day, were privileged to see the great fireball that suddenly erupted out at sea, a spectacle that none of them would ever forget.

When the fire and smoke had cleared, Captain David Fuller, through the periscope of the *Nautilus*, scanned the horizon. He smiled when he saw it. Somehow, perhaps aided by the force of the explosion behind it, the little escape capsule had outrun the *Nautilus* itself!

"Mister Pickover," said Fuller, "I think I've found your boss! Men, full speed ahead. Let's go pick him up!"

ABOUT THE AUTHOR

Aaron Smith - was born in Paterson, New Jersey in 1977. He learned to read at an early age and has never stopped. This lifelong habit of reading helped, along with films, stories told to him by his grandparents and a naturally vivid imagination to get him to start making up stories early in life. He originally wanted to be a comic book artist, but later realized that he was better suited to writing than drawing.

When asked to list the greatest influences on his writing, he would surely mention the following: Roger Zelazny, J.R.R. Tolkien, Joseph Campbell, Robert Anton Wilson, Ian Fleming, Bram Stoker, A. Conan Doyle, Jules Verne, HP Lovecraft, Stan Lee, Jack Kirby, Steve Ditko, Gene Roddenberry, Agatha Christie, Chester Gould, Alfred Hitchcock, Geoffrey Chaucer, Dante, and Homer.

His work has previously appeared in Airship 27's book, *Sherlock Holmes: Consulting Detective Volume 1*. His work will soon appear in several other Airship 27 books. *Season of Madness* is the first published book to feature only stories by Aaron Smith.

He currently resides in Clifton, New Jersey. He lives with his wife, who has the amazing ability to put up with his curmudgeonly ways and moods of incredible crankiness. He still reads a lot, watches a lot of old movies, thinks too much sometimes, and roots for the New York Yankees.

FROM AIRSHIP 27 PRODUCTIONS- THE GREAT DETECTIVE:

PULP FICTION FOR A NEW GENERATION

AN AIRSHIP 27 PRODUCTION

NEW PULP

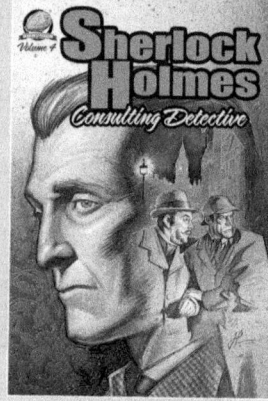

FOR AVAILABILITY OF THESE AND OTHER FINE PUBLICATIONS CHECK THE WEBSITE: AIRSHIP27HANGAR.COM

www.ingramcontent.com/pod-product-compliance
Lightning Source LLC
Chambersburg PA
CBHW071241250626
47163CB00001B/271